CRAZY
MESSY
beautiful

CRAZY

MESSY

beautiful

Carrie Arcos

Philomel Books

PHILOMEL BOOKS

an imprint of Penguin Random House LLC
375 Hudson Street, New York, NY 10014

Copyright © 2017 by Carrie Arcos.

Library of Congress Cataloging-in-Publication Data
Names: Arcos, Carrie, author. | Title: Crazy messy beautiful / Carrie Arcos. |
Description: New York, NY : Philomel Books, an imprint of Penguin
Random House LLC, [2017] | Summary: Sixteen-year-old Neruda Diaz,
influenced by his namesake, Chilean poet Pablo Neruda, yearns to fall
in love but has yet to find the right girl. | Identifiers: LCCN 2015049597
| ISBN 9780399175534 | Subjects: | CYAC: High schools—Fiction. |
Schools—Fiction. | Love—Fiction. | Bullying—Fiction. | Artists—Fiction.
| Family problems—Fiction. | Poetry—Fiction. | Classification: LCC PZ7.
A67755 Cr 2017 | DDC [Fic]—dc23 | LC record available at https://lccn.
loc.gov/2015049597

Printed in the United States of America.
ISBN 9780399175534
1 3 5 7 9 10 8 6 4 2

Edited by Liza Kaplan. Design by Jennifer Chung.
Text set in 11.25-point Fairfield LT Std.

For David

THE INFINITE ACHE

Her name was Ella. She had no other name. Ella was first, middle, and last, readily on my tongue and mind. She was older than me and a good head taller, but that didn't matter. She was my world from eight a.m. to noon, Monday through Friday.

During class, Ella pulled me, as if with an invisible string, from stuffed animals to picture books to swings to a small sandbox. I killed dragons. I rescued cats. I held babies and played house. I was the prince to her princess. We celebrated with feasts of crackers, both goldfish and graham. We shared cut-up apples and slices of oranges like they were candy. We visited outer space on secret missions. We explored uncharted lands. The truth was I would have traveled with her anywhere.

My Ella.

I can still see her—straight shoulder-length black hair, bangs like freshly cut grass across her forehead, her brown arm in a cast during those last months, wide smile with two missing front bottom teeth. Her blue flowered dress dirty from playing. Her knees red and skinned from falling off her scooter. Broken scabs scattered across to reveal smooth white scars underneath.

Like all tragic love stories, she left me . . . for kindergarten at a different school. On our last day together, Ella gave me a kiss on my cheek. I was embarrassed and ran and hid from her, refusing to come out and say good-bye.

I never saw her again.

I blame Ella. She was the one who first showed me what a terribly beautiful and cruel thing love could be. I also blame The Poet. He gave words to my anguish and made me acutely aware of this infinite ache, a deep soul longing that came sometimes in the dark and lingered in the light. His words picked at a wound I didn't even know was there until I read them. Now it's impossible to close.

But Ella . . . Ella opened my heart and then broke it. Maybe I've been trying to fix it ever since.

NUMBER EIGHT

Being named after a famous dead Chilean poet is not ideal. First of all, when you introduce yourself, everyone's like, *What?* And you have to say your name at least twice for someone to get it right.

It usually goes down like this:

"My name's Neruda."

"Wait." The person leans in closer. "How do you say your name?"

"Neruda."

"Ne . . . ru . . . da . . . interesting."

Interesting really means *weird*, but people try to be polite, unless they have no social skills at all, and then they just come out and say, "What kind of a name is that? Does it mean something?"

Of course it means something. All names have meaning, moron. My parents didn't just come up with it from a stupid Internet search either.

Then there's the occasional person who's actually heard of the name. Those people say this phrase every time: "Neruda, like the poet?"

"Yes, Pablo Neruda."

Here's the thing, though. Neruda wasn't even his real name. Pablo Neruda was actually a pseudonym for Neftalí Ricardo Reyes Basoalto. Neftalí came up with the pen name when he was a teenager to hide his writing pursuits from his dad, who wanted him to become something more practical, like a businessman or an accountant. Let's just say I'm grateful he changed his name.

Latin people have a thing for long names. It's because we take on the surnames of both parents, with the mother's name going last. You just keep adding on names. You can trace our genealogy through the last name, going back generations. Since I'm technically only half Chilean, on my dad's side, I was spared a long, complex name and am simply Neruda Wayne Diaz. The Wayne is after my mom's dad, who lives in Ohio. But to most people I'm just Neruda.

In Pablo Neruda's lifetime he wrote a ton of poems, many of them about love but also about everything in between life and death, and he was even awarded the Nobel Prize in Literature. He was also a Communist, which is always a bad thing to be if you're an American, but if you study Latin American history, you can kind of understand it. He died on September 23, 1973, twelve days after a violent military coup in Chile, way before I was born.

Every now and then I'll get a devotee, someone whose eyes flame like a zealot's when he hears my name. He'll speak to me in Neruda's words, as if I should recognize them, as if I'm Neruda reincarnate. I'm given the feverish speeches on how he was the greatest poet to have ever lived.

I know that.

You can't have a name as iconic as Neruda and know nothing about your namesake. Plus it's one of the first things my dad ever taught me. While other kids were listening to stories about moons and little pigs and cats with hats, Dad would tell me about Neruda, or "The Poet," as he referred to him. He said his own dad, my papi, who died a couple of years ago and had emigrated from Chile with his family in the 1980s, had read him Neruda when he was little too.

I don't remember Papi as well as I'd like to, and the older I get, the more my memory of him fades. When I think of him now, I can recall only a handful of things: that he liked to take

5

long walks by the ocean, do crossword puzzles, and say funny things a lot, like *"camarón que se duerme se lo lleva la corriente"*— the shrimp that falls asleep gets carried away by the current. Every time he said this, I'd imagine a little shrimp curled up in some seaweed and z's floating upward in tiny bubbles, and crack up.

He also had very strong, callused hands. We would arm wrestle, and his hands would easily dwarf mine and win. Dad never could beat him either, not even in the end.

Papi used to tell me we'd go to Chile one day so I could see where he grew up. He said we'd visit the white sand beaches and the deep green forests of our people. But he died before we got to go.

Lately I'll hear Dad muttering some of the things Papi used to. My favorite is *"Él que no encuentra el amor no encuentra nada."* He who does not find love does not find anything.

I think The Poet would agree. I'd like to think that would be his favorite too.

When I was little, Dad spoke Neruda's poetry often—some from memory, some from the worn pages of his collection passed down from Papi, most of the time in Spanish, and always underneath the soft glow of the lamp by my bed.

Dad read The Poet like English teachers read Shakespeare— with love and reverence. He has two photos on the desk in his home office. One is a picture of Mom and me from when I was six. She's hugging me from behind and I'm smiling up into the camera. The other is a picture of Papi standing next to The Poet from their chance meeting in Valparaíso just before my dad was born. So really, Neruda and his influence have been in my family for generations.

But even though I have been "Neruda, like the poet" for sixteen years, I am nothing like him. When Pablo Neruda was my age, he walked around in a large black floppy hat and black cape, seducing girls like a young Don Juan. Supposedly girls fell in and out of love with him as frequently and as easily as rain falls from the sky. Because Pablo Neruda was not just one of the greatest love poets.

He was The Greatest Love Poet of all time.

I, on the other hand, am the unluckiest in love. It's not for lack of trying. So far I'm about zero for seven, the names of the girls written on my heart like the scars I can still recall on Ella's knee—Marisol, Stephanie, Jessi, Angela, Trinity, and Elise.

I like to think of them as the preview to a great love story, one I'll hopefully get to tell—and live—someday.

Dad has told me not to worry about it. He says I'm a late bloomer and that it'll all come together for me in college, like it did for him and my mom.

But I don't want to wait.

I want to feel the passion of The Poet's words for someone

and be able to say them out loud. Lines where he talks about craving someone so much that he's become an animal, crawling and prowling the streets. Nothing can sustain him, no food, no drink, only *her*. I want to know what it is to be that hungry for someone.

And by someone, I mean Autumn Cho.

Because this is the year it's all going to change.

Eight is my lucky number.

BODY OF A WOMAN

I lean against the wall over by the math building and check the time on my phone. There's only five minutes left to get to class. I remove the small, worn-out, rolled-up book of The Poet's poems that I usually carry folded in my back pocket. It's my favorite: *Twenty Love Poems and a Song of Despair*. It's one of my dad's favorites too, and Papi's before him.

I open it to page 5 and read a few lines for inspiration, for strength. And for courage.

Autumn rounds the corner and time slows like it usually does when I see her. Today her black hair is down and she's all classic, dressed in a cream T-shirt and jeans. Even with two

9

thick textbooks underneath one arm, and a backpack, she walks with style and grace. No, she walks like she's a visitor to this world, like she's going to disappear any moment, and I'll forever wonder if I simply dreamed her up.

As she nears me, I fall in step alongside her. I turn to say hi, but she's wearing pink earbuds, so I can't get her attention.

But it's okay. This is progress.

I strut next to her, and it's like we're walking to the same soundtrack, something smooth and mellow, like an old '70s jam.

She glances at me and tosses me a smile, a real smile that makes me feel all woozy and amazing at the same time. A good smile can do that to you. And with her smile, it's like I've been waiting for it my whole life.

"Hey, Neruda," she says a little too loudly.

My name falls from her lips, and it's like she speaks me into existence. It's hers and only hers to utter. The importance of this moment, or the possible importance, hovers in the air between us. I need to mark it so that later I can trace everything back to this point on our time line—the point where we first began.

"Yeah, hey . . ." I start to say.

But she turns right and disappears into the crowd, taking the music with her. I watch in silence, not even caring about the elbows thrown my way because I'm blocking pedestrian traffic, going against the grain. Let them walk around me. They are nothing to me.

Autumn Cho is my lucky number eight. She just doesn't know it yet.

When I get to English class, Mr. Nelson's voice is all bumpy and revved up—maneuvering his volume like a speedboat hitting waves, constantly jerking forward and working hard to keep our attention.

Suddenly Callie's arm brushes up against mine on the table. This happens sometimes because I'm a lefty, and it's annoying.

Even though Callie Leibowitz sits next to me, we only interact when it's assigned. When we're forced to work together, she stares at me with a surprised, bored look, from under lids that droop with the weight of heavy black eyeliner. She's quiet in class, like me, except for when she walks. She stomps around in thick black boots with lime-green laces that rest on top like spiders. She wears those boots with everything—skirts, jeans, and shorts. Sometimes she changes the laces. I know this because I spend most of class staring down at the ground or concentrating on my drawing.

To be honest, Callie kind of scares me. She's strong both in attitude and in physicality. I've seen her on the volleyball court. Not many can return her jump serve. In fact, she'd probably take me down. I mean, not in one move, but she's got some guns on her. I can see the defined cut of her biceps when she's just sitting still. I have to work, just a little, to make mine stand out like that.

When she's not looking, I flex my arm just slightly. Then I catch her bored stare in my peripheral vision, followed by a slow grin, and stop.

I scoot over, creating even more distance between us.

Mr. Nelson is talking about some MMA fight he watched over the weekend, using it as a metaphor for life, explaining how we should work hard now because working hard in school will lead to success later in life. Mr. Nelson recycles his Motivational Speeches once a week. We've had life is like a race; life is like a football game; life is like a baby eagle that gets pushed out of the nest. He gets very animated when sharing these life lessons, knowing the class's attention span is about three minutes.

Personally, I think if Mr. Nelson really wants to keep our attention, he should flash a picture of a naked woman every now and then. Three-quarters of my group—group three—would focus for sure.

Group three is all male, except for Callie. Luis and Josh usually spend class drawing pictures of boobs and male genitalia all over their notebooks or on the desk in pen. I know when class is almost over because the last five minutes always smells like saliva and wet fingers and a feverish attempt to wipe off the drawings.

Callie goes back and forth between ignoring the drawings and giving Luis and Josh the finger.

I couldn't care less about them. The fact that my non-reaction pisses off Luis is just an added bonus.

There's nothing wrong with drawing naked bodies, but Luis's and Josh's are crude, deformed versions—fantasies of guys who probably spend a lot of time sneaking porn and have never seen a real naked female body up close.

I, on the other hand, have seen several naked women in the flesh. Over the summer, I took an art class where we studied the nude form, which is like basic training for an artist in hand-eye coordination and technique. It was hard to concentrate the first day when the female model removed her yellow robe in front of us and sat down totally naked on the stool in the center of the room. My heart was pounding so loudly, I was sure everyone could hear it, and I couldn't help being turned on. Fortunately, no one paid any attention to me. Everyone was focused on their art. By the third day, I didn't even notice the model's nakedness—well, I did notice; her body was beautiful. But I wasn't distracted by thoughts of what I'd like to do with that body. I was more concerned with capturing it on the page in all of its honest glory.

I didn't start drawing nudes right away. I first started learning how to draw in elementary school after I was diagnosed with a slight learning disability. It's been several years, but my permanent record is still marked by an "LD," tacked on to the end of my name like MD or PhD. Because of my namesake, you'd think words would be my strength.

For me, writing, especially essays, can feel like being stuck all alone in a dark cave when all you've been given to dig yourself out is a tiny plastic white spoon. I have dysgraphia, and it affects how I process information. Almost everyone knows about dyslexia because famous people have talked about it and said that even though they struggled with reading as a kid, they still went on to become a successful actor or a professional basketball player or something.

No one ever talks about dysgraphia.

Basically, if you tried to read something I wrote, you'd think two things: One, he has terrible handwriting, and two, he doesn't know anything about the English language. The first is true. I can barely read my own writing. The rest isn't, but I do have difficulty putting letters in the correct order to spell the words I mean to use, or I leave out vowels entirely, even though I think I've included them, so it can seem like I don't know how to spell or use proper grammar.

I'm also slow in the literal sense of the word. It takes me longer to process and organize. I'm not stupid, though. My reading comprehension is high. But for most people slow equals stupid, especially if you're in public school. Everything is measured by timed tests, as if how quickly you can do something signifies intelligence.

Fortunately, there are tools that can help people with dysgraphia write better. When I have a homework assignment that involves writing, I usually speak into a recorder at home. It helps me organize my thoughts. I also have this software that will type up what I'm saying. At first Mom and Dad didn't think it was a good idea—they thought that I needed to learn to write on my own. After a few months of trying harder and still getting shitty grades, a teacher in middle school explained to my parents that the software could make a real difference for someone "like me." My parents had to admit that it helped when I actually started getting better grades on writing assignments.

Still, every year I get lumped into some remedial English class (aka the "Academic Success Program!") with the other struggling students. I know it's designed to help, but it only makes me feel worse.

It's like they went, *Okay, this is everyone who sucks at the system in some way, so instead of changing the system, let's just throw everyone who sucks together so that eventually, maybe, they'll suck less.*

But it never changes. Year after year they give us the same information about how to organize our notebooks and take notes and go over how to write a thesis statement five thousand times, as if that is the real problem.

I know how to write a thesis statement. I just don't like to.

. . .

In seventh grade I had this one teacher who told me, "Neruda, there's genius inside of you. But no one's going to believe it until you show them."

The dictionary says a genius is "a very smart or talented person with great natural ability."

I am not a genius. I don't want to be a genius. It has taken me a lot of time and practice just to feel above mediocre at best. Why can't I practice and become amazing, the best in the world even, at just one thing? What makes natural ability so much better?

Without sounding conceited, I'm actually really good at drawing. Which is a good thing for someone with dysgraphia to be, because even if I can't express myself that well in words, I still have art. Plus, writing can be pretty objective; art isn't.

I keep a sketchbook with me at all times that I fill with images of lots of different things, but mostly of people. Portraits are my thing. I know this because my art teachers tell me so and keep investing. In fact, I've just been commissioned to design a mural for the school library. Mr. Fisher, my art teacher, is overseeing the project. He's got a thing for murals. I'm not really a muralist, but I'm up for the challenge. Before working on the project, I hadn't noticed how many murals there are in LA. Now I see them all the time.

If anything, I figure I can always get one of those jobs as a cartoonist at Disneyland. They probably make decent money.

. . .

From the front of the class, Mr. Nelson's voice is white noise. I'm trying to draw Callie's hand. It's in a fist on the table. Her fingers are small, with black chipped nail polish on short bitten nails. There's a hangnail, red and raw, on the side of her pointer. Her thumb has a ring that looks like an elephant, the trunk circling her finger to form the band. Two freckles dot her pinky just under the cuticle.

Luis taps at the table with a different pen, which is loud and annoying. We've been in class together off and on since freshman year PE, and he has been annoying me ever since.

During the swimming unit, we had to shower afterward. As if that wasn't enough, Luis would steal people's towels just to be a jerk. We'd find them stuffed in the trash or rolled up on top of the lockers. Then he'd laugh and say, "We're cool, right?" like we were in on the joke. It was never a joke for me.

Two years later and Luis has found new ways to be an asshole. Like sketching a woman's breasts and waving his hands in front of me until I look over. I can't help but glance at them. They look like large, round bug eyes. They're so terrible and ugly and not at all like a woman's breasts. There's no artistry in them, no flesh, no beauty. The worst is that there's no imagination.

I ignore him and Luis grabs my sketchbook. He opens it, flipping around.

"Give it back," I say.

He stops at a drawing of Autumn I did last week. It isn't complete—most of the sketches in the book aren't. They're whatever I can get done in the short amount of time that I spend watching the subject. Autumn had been sitting with her back against the brick wall near the front of school, earbuds in, legs folded in front of her and talking on the phone.

Luis shows Josh. Josh laughs that stupid idiot SpongeBob kind of laugh.

"Gentlemen, eyes up here, please," Mr. Nelson says.

I glare at Luis, trying to get him to give me back my book. Instead, Luis just folds his hands over the page and stares up at Mr. Nelson.

If Luis were a day, he'd be Monday at 7:05 a.m.

Mr. Nelson starts speaking again. Luis smirks at me and then draws the same huge balloon boobs on Autumn's picture, defiling more than just my work. He defiles my Autumn.

Something within me rises to the surface. I reach across the table, grab Luis's shirt, pull him in, and hit him. Suddenly we're on the floor and I'm on top of him. I think I climbed over the desks.

Soon everyone's yelling, or maybe it's just me. There's a scream that echoes in my brain until someone bigger and stronger tears me off of Luis—or maybe it's Luis off of me—because now I'm in some kind of hold, pushed up against the wall.

"Are you done?" Mr. Nelson asks, red-faced.

I don't answer him. Mostly because I'm afraid of what I'll say.

"He's crazy," Luis says, holding his neck. "I was just sitting there. I didn't do anything."

"Everyone stay where you are," says Mr. Nelson.

The class is watching me, so I try to control my shaking.

Then Mr. Nelson makes me walk out of the classroom like I'm some kind of criminal.

LEANING INTO THE AFTERNOONS

Principal Jones sits behind a big desk adorned with a line of superhero action figures. But the characters are all wrong. He's combining the universes—Marvel intermixed with DC characters—as if there's no order. He wants to know why I attacked Luis. I stare at Batman and Deadpool, because how do I explain a bastard like Luis?

How do I say that he desecrated my artistic expression? How do I explain love? How do I tell him that Mr. Nelson's class is soul-sucking and I was afraid that the longer I stayed there, the more I might die slowly and without honor?

If I'm going to die in this crappy school, I want to die nobly.

The principal asks me again about Luis. I just shrug.

He says that since I don't have a history of violence, he's going to give me an in-school suspension for the rest of the day and that's it. He says it could be much worse; I could have been given an actual suspension that would have gone on my permanent record. Then he asks if I have anything to add.

I don't.

The office assistant escorts me down the hall.

When I enter the room designated for in-school suspension, the middle-aged man in a red Adidas shirt and gray sweatpants points to the rules on the board, the sign-in sheet, and an empty desk.

I scan the room and don't see anyone I recognize. I'm not supposed to be here.

After I sign the paper, I move to my seat.

I get a text.

Crap. My mom. The school must have called her about my little incident.

Are you okay?

Yes

What were you thinking?

Can't text, I type, though this isn't true. Despite the "no electronic devices" rule, everyone in the room is on their phone. Tell u later.

Oh, we will talk later, that's for sure. And don't forget dinner.

Gt it covered, I text her back.

It's Monday, one of my nights to "cook." Tonight I planned bacon grilled cheese sandwiches, a salad, and tomato and red pepper soup from Trader Joe's. Piece of cake.

I check my email and see I've got one from Ezra.

Neruda,

You asked me once what I'd want to do when I got out, but I didn't answer you. I didn't want to think about it. Expectations can be a deadly thing. But now that I'm out, I can say they're simple things too. I want to see the ocean. I can count on one hand the times I've been there. Can you believe that? Never had the time to go before. I want to drive cross-country and visit every state. I want to find the best taco stand in East LA. I want to go camping and sleep outside in the open, somewhere without four walls staring at me all the time. I want my life to matter. There's so many things I want that I'm afraid if I write all of them down, I'll explode from the wanting. You ever feel that way?

This might sound strange, but here's a truth that comes in the dark. The ugliest, hardest, meanest

men cry when they think no one can hear. They
would be ashamed if they knew others could hear,
but through all these years, I've clung to that sound
because it gives me hope. Makes me realize we
are all the same in the middle of the night, fighting
against the great tide of loneliness that threatens to
drown us. All longing for someone to hear, to truly
know us as we are.

Thanks for knowing me.

See you soon.

Ezra

Ezra and I have been writing each other for three years,
since I was in the eighth grade, when Mrs. Dutton, my English
teacher, made us write letters to prisoners. She said it would
allow us to practice letter writing in a "fun and different" way,
and also help the prisoners feel a little less lonely. Mrs. Dutton's
brother was serving time for robbery, so that's why she was especially sensitive to the plight of people in prison. She told us that,
on average, most friends and family stop visiting their loved ones
in prison after three years. She had a list of prisoners we could
write to, having already screened them to see who'd want to be
pen pals with thirteen-year-olds. By the time it was my turn to
choose, Ezra Hernandez was the only name left on the page.

You have to write real letters to people in prison. They don't have personal laptops or smartphones. No email or text messaging. I sent Ezra a short note because, back then, my writing sucked even more. I had to spell-check it a bunch on the computer first to make sure it was perfect, then copy it word for word. I didn't want him thinking I was an idiot.

The letter I sent was only one line long, questioning whether light is the same for both convicts and those who are free. It was a question from The Poet's *Book of Questions*.

After a week, Ezra wrote me back. His letter said:

> Dear Neruda,
>   Only those who have known darkness
> can fully appreciate the light.
>   Sincerely,
>   Ezra Hernandez

We've been writing once a week ever since.

Even though Ezra and I talk frequently and about all kinds of things, he's not an open book. Over the years, I've teased out bits and pieces of his story. From what I can tell, he was trying to help his brother, Rafa, and ended up going with him to rob a house. I think Ezra was trying to stop him from doing it. The house was supposed to be empty, but it wasn't. Rafa was shot and killed and Ezra was sent to prison. He was eighteen at the time and served ten years for an armed robbery conviction. But as soon as I got to know Ezra, I immediately doubted his guilt. He just didn't seem like the typical stereotype of a Mexican guy in jail, the one you see portrayed on TV shows and movies—shaved head, arms covered in tats, maybe even one circling his neck or a teardrop close to his eye.

Even still, I was surprised when Ezra showed up at my door a couple of months ago looking like some fashion model with his tapered jeans and suspenders, his dark curly hair styled in a perfect-looking mess on his head, a trimmed beard, and emerald-green-framed glasses. His arms were naked of any tattoos. Even his white shoes were cool.

First, we stared at each other awkwardly, and then he smiled and pulled me in for a big bear hug. He told me I wasn't what he expected either. He never explained what he meant.

Ezra doesn't like to talk about his prison time much, but when he does talk about it, he says that he can't focus on the past. He can't change it. He can only affect the future. I can get on board with that.

Ezra and I have become pretty close these past few years. I introduced him to The Poet, and he taught me about history—specifically World War Two—working out, politics, cars, and anything he was reading about in prison. He must've read five books a week because, he said, that's all you do in prison: read. That or work out.

Ezra is crazy smart. He got two degrees while he was in jail: one in political science, the other in business. Sometimes he wrote me letters explaining the laws of commerce. And in my letters to him, I'd always start with a paragraph about how life was on the outside. Current events and stuff. He called me his man on the street. He didn't want to get out and feel as if the world had passed him by.

Now that he's out, we don't just write letters. We email and text. Meet up for basketball or food sometimes. Whatever.

Ezra's kind of like an older brother, but without all of the older-brother baggage, and he's kind of like my best friend. He's really introspective, probably from all of those years being locked inside his own head. Even now he's always talking about how I should never take things for granted. How I should work to find the good in everything and not be afraid to dream big. That every experience, the good and the bad, can teach me something. He says we all have a choice to move forward or to let the bad stuff knock us into retreat. He used to close his letters with "onward and upward, my man, onward and upward."

I read his email one more time before I write him back. It's sloppy because I can't use the app that I speak into at school. I tell Ezra about the fight with Luis. Ezra doesn't condone fighting for dumb reasons, but he's all for defending yourself. He's even taught me some moves, which is why I knew I could rush Luis like that.

I write about how stupid high school is and how maybe I should just take my GED. Ezra won't like the last idea. I've mentioned it before and he always responds that I should stay in school. He'll want to know why I want to grow up so fast. And besides, aren't there girls?

There *is* a girl.

I picture Autumn's face, her high cheekbones dotted with small freckles and eyes like deep almonds. She's so pretty, she doesn't need any makeup. I replay the way she said my name today, her voice a little higher and louder than usual, like there was real feeling behind it. It could have been the fact that she had earbuds in, but even with that, there was definitely some emotion in her words.

Autumn is the kind of girl I know I could have a real relationship with. She's different from the others because she's not only beautiful, she's smart too. She's in AP classes, plays in the orchestra, and I'm pretty sure she volunteers to read to little kids at the elementary school. She just has something special. Everything seems brighter when she's around.

I go into my photos app and find the one I took of her yesterday. I have to zoom in a little to really see Autumn because I was trying to take the picture without her knowing. She was walking to lunch with a group of her friends. Her face is tilted toward someone, but it's in my direction, so it's like she's looking at me. Her mouth is open in a small smile.

I flip through the other photos I have of her. It's not like I have a hundred of them or anything—I'm not a stalker. I have a good, healthy six photos.

Feeling inspired, I reach in my bag for my sketchbook. It's not there.

First he defiles my picture, then he steals my sketchbook. Leave it to Luis to take advantage of an already bad situation and make it ten times worse.

I bum a couple of lined pieces of paper off the person next to me and do warm-up sketches of some mural ideas. I'm thinking a collage of faces. I'm not sure how and who yet. But Mr. Fisher wants it to be a reflection of our school. I'm sure he'll be pissed when he finds out I'm in here and not in art class, so I might as well try and be productive. Maybe I'll draw different students standing, facing forward, like they're in a lineup. I can stamp the name of our school off to the side, like we're all potential suspects stuck in lockup. Mr. Fisher would probably laugh, but it would never get past the school board.

As I continue to draw, my sketches quickly morph into portraits of Autumn. By the time the bell rings signaling that school has ended, only different versions of Autumn stare up at me. Perfect, beautiful Autumn after Autumn, and my heart aches.

NOT ONLY THE FIRE

Mom reaches across the table and pushes some of my black hair aside to get a better look at the bruise that's formed above my eye.

"You're lucky. That could have been a real shiner," she says.

"How does the other guy look?" Dad asks. He turns the music down a little, some Víctor Jara song.

"Worse," I say. I don't know that for sure, but it makes me feel better.

Dad must be missing Papi today—that's the only time he plays Jara. The songs are old, folky, and guitar driven, and Jara's deep voice is full of sadness tonight. Dad belts out the chorus in Spanish and hands Mom a glass of red wine.

He gives me a kiss on the top of my head and sits down next to me.

"What did Luis do exactly?" Mom asks.

I'm embarrassed to say, so I take a bite of my sandwich.

"You can tell us." She and Dad watch me while they eat.

That's the thing with my parents; they'll just sit there and wait for me to tell them what's going on. Since I'm an only child, they don't have anyone else to interrogate or invest in. And, as Dad would say, hiding doesn't help. Everything eventually comes to light.

I take a big drink of water. Stall. "He drew boobs all over one of my pictures and laughed about it."

"All of this is over boobs? *Adónde la viste!*" Get out of here! Dad chuckles. He sobers up when he sees my face.

"It's not just the drawings," I say. What I don't say is: It's the every day, sitting next to Luis, putting up with his crap. Hearing his comments and stupid high laugh. Listening to his loud nose breathing. Having to be in that class in the first place. All of it. "He's just a jerk."

"You'll be dealing with people like Luis your whole life. You can't go around hitting them every time they deserve it. You have to be better. To rise above, *cachai*?" Dad says.

Dad always says *cachai* when he's trying to make a point. It's like saying "you know?" or "you understand?" And sure I know, but I don't understand.

"Sometimes you have to stand for principle," I say.

"I get that, but what's principle without love?" Dad asks.

I'm not in the mood for one of his speeches about loving my enemies or whatever it is he's trying to say.

We eat in silence for a few moments. Then Mom asks, "Did you at least get a good hit in?" A sly smile creeps at the corner of her mouth.

I smile back. "Yeah." I can usually count on Mom to be on my side.

"Good. Maybe next time he'll think twice about messing with you."

Mom winks at me and pulls Dad in for a kiss.

It's weird watching them sometimes, but I'd rather have parents who are in love than not. I've been around other parents whose dislike for each other is palpable. Most of my friends' parents are divorced and remarried.

My parents met in college at some house party. Mom actually came to the party with some other guy, but that didn't stop Dad from making a move. He walked right up to her, in front of the guy, and said, *"Eres la mujer más linda que jamás he visto."* You are the most beautiful woman I have ever seen.

It wasn't the most original line. I would have added some flair. Something like, "Your beauty is like the dawn, illuminating everything and breaking me into day."

It's a line I am waiting for the right moment to use.

Regardless, Mom fell for him. They dated for two years and got married when Dad was in grad school.

"I want you to apologize to your teacher and this Luis tomorrow, first thing," Dad says.

I grunt.

"What's that?" Dad says.

"Fine," I say.

Later that night, we watch TV together. Mom's legs are curled up underneath her, snuggled up against Dad. He plays with her dark curly hair, and his bare feet, crossed at the ankles, are up on the coffee table. They've been this way as long as I can remember—not afraid to show each other affection, no matter who else is around. I used to think it was gross, but now, well, it's still kind of gross, but I can see how it might be nice too.

At some point during the show, Mom's eyes close. The sharp daytime lines that trickle from the corners soften.

Dad soon gives in too and falls asleep with his mouth open. I don't think we've ever finished a show without one of them conking out. The soft moonlight glow of the TV spills over them, sending shadows like shifting craters across their faces. I draw them in one of the sketchbooks I keep at home and make a mental note to get my other book from Luis first thing tomorrow—if he hasn't ruined it beyond repair.

I add light to the dark places underneath my parents' eyes

and on their cheeks and wonder if I'll ever be like them, if I'll ever find my one great love. It already feels like I've been searching forever.

Dad shifts his position on the couch, opens and closes his mouth, gives a heavy sigh.

A guy can hope.

THE QUESTION

When I approach Mr. Nelson's classroom the next day, he is standing outside with Luis. They're obviously waiting for me, so I take my time walking.

Mr. Nelson nods to the two of us. "Gentlemen."

Luis faces me. Since Luis's dark hair is short and spiked in the front, he can't hide the pale bruise forming underneath his right eye. I didn't realize I'd hit him that hard or even in the face. I resist the urge to grin.

I hold out my hand. "Sorry," I say.

He shakes it.

"Yeah, me too."

"Good. Now come inside and take your seats."

"Yes, sir," we both say.

"Hey," I tell Luis. "I want my sketchbook back."

"What makes you think I have it?"

I give him a look like *really?* But he just shakes his head. And I know he's telling the truth for once because he's not gloating or anything. He walks into class first; I follow slowly behind.

The other students eye my table expectantly, as if they want Luis and me to get into it again. But Luis sits with his arms crossed, and I face the board.

Mr. Nelson holds up a red tin coffee can and says, "We're going to play a little game today. I've written half of your names on pieces of paper and put them in this can. Now the other half, whose names I didn't put in here, I'm going to call you up in a moment and ask you to pick out a slip of paper and read the name you've chosen out loud. After that, I'll tell you what we're going to do."

He begins calling names in alphabetical order, starting with Callie. She stands and I notice that her maroon tights are torn in the back. She fishes around for a long time before pulling out a name.

"Traden Lee," she reads. Heads turn toward Traden's empty seat.

Mr. Nelson holds out his hand for the strip of paper. "I

didn't account for the absentees. Go ahead and pick another."

She plunges her hand back in and takes just as long, which makes Mr. Nelson sigh and remind her that class is only fifty-three minutes long.

She says, "Okay, Mr. Nelson. But all choosing takes time, you know." She pulls out a piece of paper. "Neruda Diaz."

It could be worse. I could have gotten Luis or Josh or Manny, the guy with the worst BO.

When everyone has a partner, Mr. Nelson writes on the board, *Two truths and a lie.*

Then he says, "I want you to tell your partner two truths and one lie about yourself. Then you'll each take turns guessing which one is the lie. You have ten minutes. Go."

The sound of scraping chairs and stomping feet fill the room as people move to get to their partners. I just have to swivel a little in my seat to come face-to-face with Callie.

We stare at each other. She is not going to make this easy.

"You wanna go first?" I ask her.

"Um, okay, sure." She twirls a piece of hair around her pen as she speaks, which is weird because she normally just stares straight ahead, looking angry and bored.

"One—I've been surfing in Costa Rica and Hawaii. Two— my cat died when I was eight and we had a funeral for her. I dug up her left paw and kept it hidden in a jar so I could see how long it took to decompose. Three—I'm allergic to peanuts. It was once so bad that I couldn't breathe and had to be rushed to the hospital." She cocks her head at an angle. "Which is the lie?"

"I'd like to think it was the second because, no offense, that's kind of disturbing. But that's true. And the third is also true. It's the first."

She purses her lips. "Not fair. What gave it away?"

"The lack of details and your voice. The first one you rushed, like you wanted to get through it as fast as you could. It just rang false to me. And, sorry, but you don't seem like the surfer type."

She nods slowly. "Very observant. Okay. Your turn."

I think for a moment. "One—last year I was bit by a rattle-snake when we went hiking in Joshua Tree. It hurt like hell, and I still have a scar above my right ankle. Two—my best friend is an ex-convict who has spent the last ten years in prison. Three—I used to run track in middle school and always wanted to be a sprinter, but I was better at long distances, the eight hundred in particular."

She stares into my eyes. For the first time I notice hers are sandy brown with golden flecks fanning out from the irises. Her lids are rimmed in blue and there is glitter on them. I try to memorize the texture and colors so I can draw them later.

"The second one's the lie." She sits back and folds her arms over her chest, certain of it.

"Time's up," Mr. Nelson says.

"Truth," I say.

WHO ARE YOU

"So, how many of you were able to guess the lie?" Mr. Nelson asks.

I raise my hand along with only a few other people. I'm surprised. Most people are horrible liars.

"You guys come to class every day, sit next to the same people, share the same space. But how many of you really know one another?"

As I look around the room, the answer is clear: not at all. I know a few things because, like Callie said, I'm observant. Like, I know that Josh wears the same shoes every day, thick black sneakers with a worn-off label. I know that Isobel is dating Marcel; he always drops her off at the door and gives her a good-bye hug. I know that Ernie has a speech impediment, so he sits like a ghost in the back of the room and tries to disappear. And Luis, well, I know Luis more than I'd like to. I could probably offer one small fact about almost everyone in the room, but not much more beyond a one-line description. And no one knows me.

"I think my experiment today proves that most of you don't really know one another at all. So here's your assignment."

There's immediate chatter and the shifting of bodies in seats.

"I'd like you to do a research project on your partner. It is up to you to determine what angle you want to write it from, but I'd like you to go a little deeper than simply where they're from and how many siblings they have. You'll want to generate some questions and interview each other. For example . . ."

He turns to the whiteboard and writes with the red marker.

"What's the thing that scares you the most? If you could only save three possessions from a fire, what would they be? What's your favorite childhood memory?"

"Can we switch partners?" Josh yells out.

Shannon, his partner, says, "Yes, please?"

"Nope. That's why you randomly picked the person. Call it fate. You are supposed to get to know this person. Now I want you to spend some time creating ten unique questions of your own. You can only steal one of mine." He puts on some classical piano music, which is supposed to relax us and help us focus.

Callie and I start with Mr. Nelson's question about our biggest fears. Well, I have to start because she's just sitting there. Silent.

"For me, I would hate to be eaten alive."

She nods. "Typical. Which animal?"

"Shark. It's why I don't really enjoy swimming in the ocean. Shark attacks are rare, but they still happen."

"Yeah, but hippos are actually more dangerous than sharks. And lions and cheetahs," she says.

"But we don't have any of those here."

"I'm just saying if you're in Africa. Anyway, I hate those manholes. Every time I see one, I have to walk around it. It probably sounds totally irrational, but I've always been terrified of things hiding down there."

"Like rats?"

"No, more like evil aliens or huge slimy creatures. They're plotting how to come to the surface and kill us all. Actually, if we combine our fears—being eaten alive by zombies hiding inside a manhole—that would be the worst."

Callie seems totally sincere, so I nod, even though horror movies aren't my thing and she is clearly crazy.

"Because they're alive and their intestines are spilling out and they're screaming." Callie doesn't sound repelled by the killings at all. She sounds lit up by them.

"We've probably got a better chance of being hit by a car than having to deal with a zombie apocalypse," I say.

"My cousin was killed by a drunk driver last year."

I feel like a jerk and don't know what else to say, so I spend the last of our ten minutes drawing a street with a manhole. Callie watches silently as I create a blob oozing out of the top of it.

"Okay, class," Mr. Nelson says. "Time's up for now. Make sure you get your partner's contact information so you can meet up outside of class. Since this is a research project, you aren't going to get time to work on it here."

He actually seems giddy, like this is some big social experiment that will forever change our lives or something. He doesn't realize that most people will wait until the day before it's due, talk for fifteen minutes on the phone or at lunch, and write the paper that night.

Callie and I stand up and exchange our numbers. She takes my information with the same slightly bored stance she always has in class, leaning against the desk.

I start to turn away when she says, "So, you never told me your lie."

"Oh. The rattlesnake bite. I've never been to Joshua Tree." She nods.

I try to get one more good look at her eyes, for drawing purposes.

"What?" she asks.

"Nothing," I say, and look away.

"Oh, I almost forgot." She reaches into her bag. "Here."
She hands me my sketchbook.

I stare at her. Why does she have it?

"Uh, thanks," I say, holding it to my chest, suddenly feeling exposed.

"I looked through it."

"Whatever." I flip through the pages out of instinct. Everything looks the same as before.

"You really draw everything. I saw my hand on the table in there."

"Oh yeah, I was just—"

"It was good. You're really good at drawing people."

I find the page that Luis defiled and grimace. There's Autumn's face and, beneath it, two round melon-sized breasts. "I didn't make the, you know, I didn't—"

"What, the boobs? Yeah, I figured. Autumn is pretty and nice. We had a class together last year."

"She was just sitting there, so, you know, I didn't have anything else to draw."

Callie gives me a small smile as if to say *yeah right*. I've never seen her smile before.

"By the way, I was happy you kicked his ass. Luis. He needed it," she says.

"I just caught him by surprise."

"No, you had some moves. And he's a good wrestler, so that's no easy thing."

I shrug.

She throws her backpack over her shoulder. "Do you have trouble taking compliments?"

"I don't know." I don't normally get compliments, well, except from Mr. Fisher about my art. And from my parents.

"You're deflecting. That's what my therapist calls it."

"You have a therapist?"

Callie starts walking toward the door, and I follow her outside. It's loud and crowded with the lunchtime rush of students. I have to walk closely to match her pace and lean in a little to hear what she's saying.

"After I walked in on my mom sleeping with my ex—I kind of freaked out. I broke tons of things, threatened to hurt myself." She holds out her arm, showing a scar across her left wrist that I hadn't noticed before. "Anyway, Mom moved out and Dad sent me to therapy. It's not bad, it's just . . . weird."

Callie doesn't stop walking until she reaches one of the few trees on campus and stands beneath it. She faces me. "How did I do?"

"What?" My head's still spinning from her confession.

"Did you believe me?"

"Wait, that was all made up?"

She grins again and watches my face intensely, which makes me stumble backward a little.

"Very good," I say.

"I worked on the details."

"That was fast."

"Not now—while we were doing the questions. I'm actually pretty slow. I 'can't finish tests in the allotted time,'" she says, using air quotes, her voice switching to that of a formal evaluation. "I also 'can't answer a question about what I've read on the fly, can't organize' . . . and so on."

I nod. I'm very familiar with the concept of being a slow test taker.

"So your mom . . ."

"Oh yeah, no, she didn't sleep with my ex. She's actually a therapist herself. Try growing up with someone who's always making you go deep and find the root behind why you do things."

Callie plops down on the ground. Mel and Imogen walk up arm in arm. I've seen them on the volleyball court with Callie.

"Hey," Mel says.

"Hi," says Imogen.

Mel is also in my math class. Imogen is in the manga club. I joined two years ago because it's basically all girls. I'm not proud. I'll admit I was desperate. I joined because of Elise, my number seven. But Elise ended up liking Ben, the only other guy in the group, and I didn't care enough to keep up with all the books and the meetings. The manga club is very serious about their books and culture.

Mel and Imogen sit down across from Callie. They've all got that long-legged athletic gracefulness to them that volleyball players have. I feel awkward hovering above them. They take out their lunches, and I pretend I'm scanning the quad for someone.

As if on cue, Autumn crosses my line of sight, the sunlight following her like a spotlight through the crowd. I consider shouting her name, watching as she turns, running across the quad to meet her. We embrace and I throw her back and plant a kiss on her right in front of everyone, but we don't care because all we can see is each other.

I'm lost in this thought when Callie's question brings me back down.

"So, when are we going to meet up?" she asks.

"Whenever," I say, watching Autumn get farther away, trying to figure out what excuse I can come up with to talk to her.

"How about Friday?"

Just as fast as she appears, Autumn disappears. Darn it.

I glance down at Callie. She's shielding her face from the

sun, waiting for my answer. Her beat-up black boots point in my direction. Today her laces are white with black skulls and crossbones. The symbol of death.

"Friday? Sure, that'll work. Later."

I take off in Autumn's direction.

I HUNT FOR A SIGN
OF YOU

I find Autumn sitting outside on the ground by the band room. She's by herself and eating a burrito. I wonder if it's a bean-and-cheese or if she's a chicken or beef kind of girl. She looks like spring today in her multicolored flowered top and jeans. I take out The Poet's book from my back pocket and walk over to her.

"Hi, Autumn."

She removes one of her earbuds and squints up at me. "Yeah?" Even with half of her face all scrunched up, she's adorable.

"Hi."

"Hi."

We do away with the formalities pretty quickly and I'm left standing there in front of her. Standing anywhere near Autumn Cho is a privilege and awesome really, so I don't mind that she starts to look in every direction but the one I'm standing in.

"Is that your clarinet?" I point to the black clarinet case resting at her side. When she finishes chewing, Autumn responds.

"Yep."

"You have band practice today?"

"Yep."

Autumn is very succinct.

"You guys play all the classics, right?" I rack my brain for the ones I know. "Mozart, Beethoven, Shopen . . . Shopennagun?" I fudge the third name because I don't actually remember it.

"Charlie Parker," she says. "We're a jazz band."

"Oh yeah." I nod. "Jazz." Be bold, I tell myself. "So, I wanted to pass this along to you." I hold out the book to her. She eyes it suspiciously.

"What is it?"

"Just a book of poems."

"Why?"

"They're really good. I think you'll like them."

"Okay." Autumn takes the book and puts it in her bag.

"Great." I smile, glad to have gotten to this point with her. Only now I have no idea what to say to her next.

Pause. "Thanks," she says.

"Sure." Another pause.

"So, um, happy reading," I say.

Autumn puts her earbud back in, and I turn to leave.

I let The Poet work his magic.

Advanced Art is my last period of the day and my saving grace in school. My friend Greyson high-fives me when I enter class. He and art class are about the only things that make school bearable.

Mr. Fisher begins with some pointers on working with oils and then he sets us loose. I suppose walking in would be a bit of a shock for someone expecting a typical high school classroom, because it's super quiet. Most students have their earbuds in.

"Check it out," Greyson says to me, and motions me over to his canvas. He pulls off the cover. "Thoughts? You can tell me for real."

He's obviously worked on his painting at home, because it's way further along than it was the last time he showed me.

Greyson's creating a three-piece series exploring what lurks in the shadows of our subconsciousness. Piece two, what he's currently painting, has body parts all over, hacked and misshapen and oozing blood that pools into the heads of two little anime-styled children with long purple and pink hair. Very dark. Very creepy. Very Greyson.

"It's awesome."

"Yeah?" Greyson says this like he's not sure, but it's all an act. Greyson knows how talented he is. And I respect him for that. Our styles are way different, but there's mutual admiration for sure. It's why we are friends and have been since we first sat next to each other in Beginning Art years ago.

"Mr. Yang, I'm not sure if I should commend you or have you committed," Mr. Fisher says, suddenly standing there behind us.

"So, you like it?" Greyson asks.

We wait for a response from Fisher. Sometimes the waiting can be long; other times, he makes his opinion known right away. Today it's a long silence. But then he gives the nod. It's a subtle shift to the left. But it's enough.

Full-blown smile from Greyson.

Fisher turns his attention to my work next. "Mr. Diaz, I'm not sure you know what you want to say yet."

He's right. I'm struggling. Part of it is the medium. Part of it is I'm not fully invested.

I stare at my painting. In the center is a boy I saw sitting on the curb in front of a Salvadoran restaurant. He was playing on his device and totally oblivious to everything around him. I liked how his stillness was such a contrast to the busy intersection next to him. I keep referring to the quick sketch I made at the time, but I can't seem to capture the boy's essence.

Greyson's piece has an urgency and emotion to it—also a violence. Compared to his painting, mine looks amateurish.

I know to be patient when it comes to creating a piece of art. It's not the outcome that matters; it's the trying. I'll only get better through failure. Because each time I fail, I learn and I change so that every time I get closer to creating what I see in my head.

This is Mr. Fisher's mantra. But it's still frustrating when I can't execute my vision successfully.

Mr. Fisher gives me some pointers and then moves on to someone else.

"You could let his eyes kind of droop out of their sockets. That'd be cool," says Greyson.

"No, that would be you."

He shrugs. "It'd still be cool."

We work next to each other in quiet, but I'm too frustrated and distracted to make much more progress. I keep thinking of Autumn and what she'll say about the book.

After a couple of attempts to be productive, I cover the portrait back up and work on my ideas for the school mural in my sketchbook.

Greyson glances at my drawings. "I don't know why Fisher didn't ask me to do the mural."

"Umm . . . exhibit A." I point to the severed neck of one of the anime girls he's been working on. "Besides, you don't have time."

Since Greyson joined water polo and started an internship at his dad's architecture firm, I hardly see him myself. We used to hang out every other weekend.

"True," he says. "Mercy complains about that."

Mercy. Greyson's girlfriend since the summer.

"I don't have practice today, though," he says. "Want to come over?"

"Sure."

After school at Greyson's house, we eat some leftover pizza in the fridge. I debate about telling Greyson that I gave Autumn the book. I know he will probably roll his eyes and laugh at me. He doesn't approve of my methods. In his defense, they haven't actually worked. Yet. And even if he is the one with a girlfriend, it's not a level playing field. Greyson is confident. Greyson always knows what to say. He's funny and popular and girls always like him.

I decide not to say anything for now.

Then we grab some sodas and chips and head for his room. We've been playing *Call of Duty* Capture the Flag for about twenty minutes when he says, "I'm thinking of ending it with Mercy."

"Why?"

I launch a smoke grenade and take off from behind some shrubbery.

"Too many expectations. Did I tell you that she got all pissed because I didn't text her back right away last week?"

"No."

"And it's not like I'm sitting around. Between work, school, sports, and everything, I just can't see her like she wants. I barely have time to see my friends, you know?"

"True."

"I don't know . . . she's great and everything, but it's getting complicated."

"Complicated doesn't mean it's not worth it," I say.

The only time Greyson and I have deep talks is when we play video games.

"Did you see how hot Jasmine looked today?" he asks as he shoots up a bunch of guys.

Jasmine is a foreign exchange student from Singapore. Greyson talks about her a little too much for a guy who is supposed to be in a relationship.

"Yeah. She was all right."

"All right? Oh, wait, you were probably too busy putting in the work for Autumn."

Putting in the work is what Greyson calls anything having to do with girls.

"Shut up," I say.

"Did you actually talk to her today?"

"Maybe."

"No shit?"

"I gave her The Book."

He laughs. "Wow."

"Shut up," I say again.

"When has The Book ever worked?"

"Doesn't mean it won't," I mumble.

Greyson's man grabs the flag and I lose.

"Damn," I say.

"For your sake, man, I hope something happens soon."

The next day, one of Autumn's friends hand delivers the book to me. There's a small note inside.

> Neruda, how weird that you have the same name as this poet. Coincidence? Anyway, thanks for the book. It was good. I hope that I'm not assuming something, but I feel like I should be honest with you. I think you are a nice guy, but I don't like you in that way. I'm sorry. Thank you again, and I hope I didn't hurt your feelings.
>
> Autumn

I read the note over a couple of times. The words *I don't like you* expand and erupt in my heart with each reading.

I try to write a response, but I can't form the words. I literally can't get my pen to cooperate with my brain. My words mark the page as if a second-grader has written them—crooked and misspelled.

My heart spends the rest of the day in the shadow of Autumn's letter. For consolation, I read "XX," by The Poet, which begins: "Tonight I can write the saddest lines." It's about a girl who doesn't return a boy's love, and the pain and the loneliness are more real to me now. It's like the poem was written especially for me, and the girl he speaks of is Autumn.

I crumple up her letter and throw it in the trash.

GIRL LITHE AND TAWNY

On Friday night I'm still crushed by Autumn's rejection, but I head over to Callie's to work on our research project. I park my red Vespa scooter on the curb in front of her house, and just as I remove my helmet, Callie opens the front door. She comes down the walkway and leans against the rail, watching me. She looks different somehow.

"Yours?" she asks, referring to the scooter.

"Yeah, birthday present last year." At first I was worried that a scooter would reflect poorly on my manhood, but when it became clear that a car was nowhere in the conversation, I accepted the present and can now admit to its usefulness. Dad said it would build my character to have to work for a car. So far I have more character saved up than money.

"Cool. I got a fifty-dollar gift card to H&M," she says with what sounds like disappointment.

I don't know what H&M is, but I figure it's bad the way she says it. "That sucks," I say.

She shrugs. "It's all good. I bought some needed basics and accessories. Come on in."

Seeing Callie outside of school is weird, but what's weirder is that she's not wearing her big black boots. The weirdest thing of all, though, is just how normal and almost nice she's being. I follow her bare feet through the front door. Her feet cross the wood floor like a cat's—deliberately and without sound.

"Welcome to Casa Leibowitz. Mom, Dad, Neruda's here!" she yells as we enter.

She leads me down the hall, past a dining table, and into a large living room with a gray sectional sofa that takes up most of the space. A woman who looks like an older version of Callie with darker, shorter hair sits at one end of the couch. A man with gray hair and a maroon hoodie sits on the other end. Both are wearing headphones and working on laptops when we enter, so they don't even look up or seem to hear us.

Callie stands in front of her mom to get her attention.

Her mom removes her headphones, sets the computer down, and stands up. After a moment, her dad does the same.

"Guys, this is Neruda."

"Hi." I shake both of their hands. Her mom and I are eye level, but her dad towers over all of us, which is not intimidating at all. I rock on my heels and put my hands in my back pockets.

"Neruda, like the poet?" her dad asks.

"Yes, sir."

"Studied him in college." Callie's dad spreads his stance and crosses his arms in front of him. "I bet your parents are writers, huh?"

"Actually, no, my mom is an actuary. My dad loves poetry, though. He's an English professor."

"Where does he teach?"

"USC," I say.

Callie's dad smiles wide at his wife and puffs himself up.

"Don't you start," she tells him.

"Mom went to UCLA," Callie explains.

But she doesn't really have to. The USC and UCLA rivalry is pretty well known all over LA. Even though Dad teaches at USC, I'm not biased. For the money factor alone, I get why people choose UCLA. I'd get a huge discount on tuition at USC, but it's not like I'll get in. You practically need a GPA of 4.5 plus extracurriculars. I'd be lucky just to get into Cal State. But I'm thinking I might apply to more of an art school instead of a traditional college anyway, somewhere like the Art

Center in Pasadena or even Rhode Island School of Design.

"I'm always fascinated by the history of names," her mom says, bringing the conversation back to me.

"I'm named after a girl who died from cancer when they were kids. That's not heavy at all," Callie says.

Her mom reaches out and pulls on a piece of Callie's brown hair. "She was my best friend. And Callie means 'beautiful,' so there's that too."

"Mom," Callie says.

But as her mom says it, I notice that Callie does look kind of pretty. Brighter or something. I can't figure it out. Maybe it's the lighting. Maybe it's that her hair is down. Maybe it's that she's smiling.

Her parents continue to conduct their own research assignment.

"Where do you live, Neruda?" her dad asks.

"About eight minutes that way." I point left across my body, except I'm all turned around, so I have to adjust it and turn to the right. "Actually, that way."

Just then a big yellow Lab comes down the stairs, wagging its tail. It heads for me, sniffing. I bend down to pet it. "Hello there."

"Her name's Lucy," Callie says. She rubs Lucy behind the ears.

"Hi, Lucy."

"There's meat in the Crock-Pot and buns on the table if you guys want to make yourselves some sloppy joes. I think it's going to be a work-through-dinner kind of night," says Callie's mom.

"Nice to meet you," her dad says, and they resume their original positions on the couch.

Callie walks into the kitchen and I follow. She grabs a paper plate, puts a bun on it, and opens the slow cooker for the meat. I do the same. There's also a simple romaine salad with tomatoes and almonds.

"Here." Callie hands me a bottle of dressing. "They're weird, huh?" she asks as she picks out all of the cherry tomatoes from her plate and puts them back into the big salad bowl.

"No," I say. Even though she's giving me permission to insult her parents, I realize I don't want to.

"Dad's a writer and graphic designer. Mom's a marriage and family counselor."

"Cool," I say.

We take our plates of food over to the kitchen nook, where Callie has a notebook already open. I feel myself stealing glances at her. It's not just the hair. It's not just that she's actually being sort of friendly for a change.

Suddenly, it hits me. She's not wearing any makeup.

"What?" she asks.

Crap. I didn't realize I was staring.

"Nothing."

I take a bite of my sandwich. It's not bad. It's got a little kick to it. I try to focus on the flavors, try to figure out what spices her mom must have used to season the meat, but all I keep thinking is that Callie looks really pretty. Surprisingly pretty. I guess she's always been pretty in an aggressive, I-don't-need-any-help-from-a-guy kind of way. But tonight she's softer. Much more chill and easy to talk to.

"So I figure we can just eat and ask our questions. I think we should have a rule, though," she says.

"A rule?" I glance back up at her quickly, afraid if I make eye contact for too long, she'll be able to read my thoughts. I look a little to the side of her instead, but she turns around to see what I'm looking at. Then she gives me a quizzical look. I smile like a goof.

"Yeah," she says. "Like, veto power. If we don't want to answer a question, we don't have to. Period."

"Okay." I can agree to that.

"Let's get the particulars out of the way first. Like parents, siblings, ethnicity, where you're originally from, et cetera . . ."

I take a big bite of sandwich.

"I can go first if you want," Callie says.

I nod my head in agreement. Mouth full.

"Well, I already told you about Mom and Dad. I'm an only child; though they wanted more kids, it just didn't work out.

My mom's family is from New England. Dad's is from Philadelphia. I was born here. You already know Mom went to UCLA and Dad went to USC—that's why he was all pleased when you said your dad teaches there. During college football season, it gets a little crazy around here with the two of them."

"Yeah, I bet."

"Let's see . . . oh, my dad's Jewish and my mom is a European mix—Irish, English, and French. She converted to Judaism when she married Dad, but we're not the observant kind that go to synagogue on a regular basis or anything. We're more like in-name-only or the high-holiday Jews. I do believe in God, though."

She pauses for a breath and looks at me.

"Are you going to take any of this down?"

"Oh yeah, sure." I take out my phone and type some notes about her parents and her Jewish heritage.

"So, what about you?" she asks.

"My dad grew up Catholic, and there's a church down the street we go to sometimes. But we don't really practice a religion either. Except we do celebrate Easter and Christmas." I take another bite. "I believe in God too."

"Yeah, it's kind of hard not to when there's so much mystery out there," she continues. "I've been to a Catholic church before. It was really different. Do you go to confession?"

"No. But my dad grew up going on a regular basis. Actually,

when he was a kid, he thought he would become a priest. He was an altar boy and everything. But then he went to college and didn't want to. I think it had something to do with meeting my mom. We've never really talked about it."

"It's kind of a cool idea," Callie says. "Being able to say what you've done in secret to one other person and walk out feeling forgiven."

"Do Jews have confession?"

"Not to a rabbi or anything. It's more like a personal thing between you and God."

"Oh."

I wonder what Callie would ask forgiveness for. My confession would be a boring tale of white lies, small jealousies, and one moment of rage. Though my hitting Luis is something I don't believe I need to ask forgiveness for. He had it coming.

"My birthday is February twenty-first, and . . . yeah. I guess those are the basics. What about you?" Callie asks.

"Just a sec." I finish jotting down a few final notes in my phone. She talks way faster than I type. I should have recorded her instead.

"Okay, well, I'm an only child too."

"That's weird. Most of my friends have siblings."

"Hmm. Weird."

"You're probably independent, responsible, a rule follower," she says.

"I guess. For the most part." I watch her write the words down. Her handwriting is almost as bad as mine. I never really noticed before.

"My mom says it's natural for firstborns and only children to be that way. She's told me all about birth-order dynamics and stuff. It's crazy how much of our life is determined by something we have no control over."

Callie is pretty deep. Much deeper than she lets on in class.

"Yeah, not just birth order," she continues, "but parents too. Environment. Social status. Class. Ethnicity. All of it."

"We have control over how we handle it, though." I think of Ezra and how he could have wasted away in prison all those years. Instead he got two degrees, worked on himself, and became the person he wanted to be. "Like, we can choose not to let the external circumstances define us or shape us."

Callie stares intently at me, making me feel uncomfortable.

"Or something . . ." I play with my napkin.

"No, that's so true. I've never heard it put that way."

I smile.

"Where do you live?" she asks.

"In Highland Park," I continue.

"And when's your birthday?" she continues.

"December twenty-sixth."

"Ah, tough one. Right after Christmas."

"Yeah." We usually celebrate it on Christmas and it's

overshadowed, or the next day and it feels like an afterthought.

"That sucks. We do Hanukkah instead," she says. "Which I like because it's fun and it lasts for more than one day. But I'd hate to have my birthday right after Christmas. No one's ever around to hang out during the holidays."

"True," I say. "So no Christmas tree?"

"Oh, we have a tree. We also have a menorah. Mom likes to cover our bases. She didn't want me growing up feeling like I missed out on anything, so we celebrate both. She even used to hide eggs and stuff on Easter."

Considering that Callie and I have barely spoken, our conversation flows pretty well. It's weird.

"Okay!" She taps her notebook on the table. "Now for the serious questions."

"Should I be nervous?" I chuckle.

Callie eyes me but doesn't return my laugh. I quickly put up my guard and wait for the harder class version of Callie to make her appearance.

"Maybe a little," she says with a smirk. "My first serious question is, how do you like your pizza crust? Thin or thick?"

"Thin."

"Me too. Next, the mountains or the beach?"

"Mountains."

"Two for two. Okay, now this is a big one: coffee or hot chocolate?"

"Coffee," I say.

"Aww. I guess we had to differ eventually."

She's being so nice. So unlike Callie. I don't get it.

She looks at her paper and reads another question. "Okay. What's your thing?"

"My thing?"

"Yeah, you know, the thing that makes you you. Everyone has a thing. What makes you unique?"

"My drawing, I guess. Is yours volleyball?"

"Sort of."

"You're really good."

"I'm okay. Not as good as Imogen. Volleyball is one of my things, but not *the* thing."

"So then what's your thing?"

For the first time all evening, Callie hesitates, like she's still deciding whether or not to tell me. After a few seconds, she puts her pen down. "Come on. I'll show you."

We climb the narrow stairs to the top floor of the house. Her bedroom is the third door on the left. There's a large bed with an orange covering and tons of multicolored pillows. She heads to a desk with a mirror and a stool in front of it. The walls are covered with female models from magazines and old movie posters, mostly horror or monster films like *Night of the Living Dead* and *The Exorcist*. There's also *The Wizard of Oz*, which seems a little out of place. A Korean flag hangs from a corner.

"What's with the flag?"

"I do tae kwon do."

She does martial arts? Figures. "What're you, some black belt?"

"Oh no, I'm terrible at it. My parents just wanted us to do something together. My master keeps passing me on because of my good attitude and work ethic. Tae kwon do is more about discipline than physical strength."

"Ah, so you can't break boards with your bare hands?"

"Oh, I can break *a* board, just not more than one. Mom is pretty awesome at it, though. Too bad I didn't inherit her skills."

I scan all the volleyball and swimming trophies on her bookshelf.

"Didn't know you were a swimmer."

"Not so much anymore, but I used to be."

She's got the broad shoulders of a swimmer.

A stack of magazines make a pile on the floor, and more cutout pictures of models are pinned up on the mirror and splayed across the bed.

"So . . . you collect photos from magazines?"

"They're more like for research and inspiration." She removes a clipping off the mirror on her desk. "I'm working on this right now."

It's a Japanese model with blue and purple hair in a wedge

cut with long strands hanging down in front. Her cheeks are purple, too, along with her eyelids and lips. She looks a little freaky.

Callie holds the photo next to her face. "What do you think?"

I know she's asking about the picture, but all I can focus on is Callie. I suddenly feel like drawing her. My fingers actually twitch.

Before I can reply, she says, "I'm going to try this over the weekend." She studies the photo. "I mean, I know I don't look anything like the model, and her cheekbones are amazing, but I just love all the color. It's so bold."

She opens her makeup kit, revealing rows and squares of colors and brushes.

"Wow. Do you design your own, um—faces?"

In response, Callie pulls out a photo book and shows me a picture where one half of her face is covered in orange and black makeup, like she's a leopard. I flip over to the next page, where the bottom half of her face and neck are covered in all different shades of aqua, making it look like she's coming out of water. The next shows a checkered pattern of red, green, and black covering her whole face. Her eyes pop out because she's wearing green contacts.

"These are amazing," I say.

"Thanks. I was bored one day and just started playing around. I haven't really showed anyone."

"Why not? You're really good."

She shrugs and goes to close up the book, but I take it from her so I can look through the photos more slowly.

"Why makeup?"

"I don't know. I guess I like that you can become anything or anyone you want. Don't you ever wish sometimes that you were someone else?"

It's a good question, one I don't really want to answer because the answer feels so obvious, it's embarrassing.

Callie runs her fingers across the face of the model and says, "I do."

Maybe it's because she's home and comfortable, or maybe it's because she's dressed very casually, but Callie seems so much more open and vulnerable than she ever does at school. It feels like she's inviting me to ask her more about herself, beyond the assignment, and encouraging me to reveal more about myself too. If I were someone with a little more courage, maybe I would say, *Yes, I'd like it if I had a little more luck in the love department.* But I'm not going to say that to Callie. I don't want her to think that I'm this desperate loser who can't get a girl. Not that it matters what she thinks.

The one who matters, Autumn, has basically crushed my ego and my heart. Autumn, who I'll have to add to my list of failed paramours. Just thinking about her makes my chest ache a little. Why is love so cruel?

I turn my focus back to Callie. "What inspires you? When you're doing your faces, I mean."

"Sometimes it's a dream or a feeling. That was from a nightmare I had about this monster fish with big teeth." She points to a photo where her eyes are closed and her face is taken over by a huge mouth of white jagged teeth, outlined in gray.

"You're an artist," I say.

"You sound surprised."

"No—well, yes. I thought you were more of a sports girl."

"Can't someone be both?"

"Sure." And I realize I don't know anything about Callie. Nothing that matters, anyway.

She juts out her chin in defiance. "Hopefully I'll be a makeup artist one day, but not just in a MAC store—for fashion shows or even film."

"I didn't know makeup could be like this," I say.

"Like what?"

"Like a work of art. I thought makeup was, you know, something girls wore to look older and women like my mom wear to look younger." I stare at the last photo, at the thorny rose vines that wrap around her neck and face and down the side of her left arm. She's crazy talented.

"Makeup is art," she says, "but I can't do what you do in that book of yours."

"You probably could if you studied. I'm mostly good at

portraits, but I just started using oils in Fisher's class. It's such a different medium. All the bold color."

"I love color."

"I can tell."

She studies me for a moment. "You're different than I thought," she says.

"What do you mean?"

"In class you're just so quiet. You never really talk to me. You seem kind of mad or indifferent or something. And you hardly move. I've watched you. You sit so still—like one of your drawings. Sometimes I want to poke you just to make sure you're not dead."

I'm shocked. It's true I don't talk to Callie, but I don't really talk to anyone. And it's not like she talks to me either. But it's the admission that she watches me that comes as a much greater surprise.

"I hate that class," I say.

"Yeah, me too."

"You should see me in Algebra II," I say. "I'm all smiles."

She laughs. "I bet."

"You're different too," I say.

"Yeah? How?"

I shrug. I don't want to say that she's actually nice or that she feels more human, like she's not going to glare at me and give me the finger. Instead, I glance around the room. "You like old movie posters. And . . ." I point to the poster of some guy with the caption *Hey girl* . . .

She laughs. "Oh, come on. Who doesn't have a crush on Ryan Gosling? Anyway, some of the movie posters were my dad's and I grabbed them for the vintage factor. But I only took the ones with the best makeup and costuming. I love movies. Have you seen any of these?" She switches gears quickly and directs my attention to the rest of the posters.

"No."

"Not even *The Wizard of Oz*?" She says it like I've missed out on something essential in my childhood.

"No. I've heard of it, I've just never seen it."

"We have to remedy that right away. How long can you stay?"

"I don't have plans."

"Cool. Tonight your mind will be blown. I'm taking you to Oz."

"What about our questions?"

"We've got the basics covered for now. Some things are more important in life."

As Callie gets the popcorn ready, I look up Ryan Gosling on my phone. If any two people are physical opposites, it's Ryan Gosling and me. First of all, he's a white guy with blondish hair. I'm Latino with brown skin and brown eyes and thick, dark, wavy hair with a close fade on the sides.

Ryan stands posed with his shirt off, revealing his six-pack abs. I barely have any definition. I make a mental note to begin a routine of sit-ups tomorrow morning. I don't need Callie to find me attractive, but hopefully someday someone will. And reading the comments under Gosling's name, I see he's popular with the ladies.

We watch the movie on the living room couch, a bowl of popcorn between us. After her parents also got over the shock that I'd never seen *The Wizard of Oz*, they disappeared somewhere upstairs.

When the movie starts in black and white, I brace myself for a slow, boring story. The sets are all so fake, but after the tornado hits and Dorothy steps into color, I have to admit I'm kind of into it. It's probably due more to the fact that I'm sitting so close to Callie in the dark than the movie itself. I've never watched a movie alone with a girl before.

Dorothy is skipping down the yellow brick road with the Scarecrow when Callie and I reach into the bowl at the same time.

"Oops," I say.

"Sorry," she whispers, and pulls away.

I remain still as a tree the rest of the night with my arms folded across my chest, nervous that we'll touch again. Nervous because I can't ignore how oddly good it felt to do so. I tell myself to get a grip. This is Callie. Black-boot-stomping

Callie. Scary. Tons-of-makeup Callie. Not my type at all. Then Autumn's pretty face comes to mind and I relax. Autumn is definitely my type. Even if she doesn't think she's interested in me.

Callie gives commentary throughout. She tells me facts about the movie, like how an actor cast as the Tin Man developed aluminum toxicity from the makeup and was forced to drop out of the film, and the guy they replaced him with, who did star in the movie, got an eye infection as a result of the makeup. She explains how the Wicked Witch's makeup could not be ingested, so the actress lived on a liquid diet throughout production. She also tells me that you can see the Witch leaving through a trapdoor in one scene and pauses the movie to show me.

"Wow," I say. "Cool."

Callie is like a movie historian.

"I know, right? From the first time I saw this movie, all I've ever wanted to do is makeup and costuming. I think I was about seven."

I try to picture a seven-year-old Callie.

"This one year, I went as the Wicked Witch for Halloween, and my mom freaked because I used real green paint. It took forever to get off my skin."

I laugh.

At the end of the movie, Dorothy returns home and is surrounded by her loving family, though I'm not sure if we're supposed to think it was all a dream or not.

"That was pretty good," I say.

"Yeah, I love that it really holds up, even after all this time. Today, Dorothy would be caught in a love triangle with the Tin Man and the Cowardly Lion," she says, "but she would have run off with the Good Witch and made her way to LA, where they would have signed on for their own reality TV show and wound up hating each other."

"A little cynical there."

"Maybe." Callie stands up and takes the empty bowl to the kitchen. I follow behind.

"I don't know," I say. "The world needs more happy endings, don't you think?"

"Sure, but that's not reality. Most of the time things don't all work out in the end."

"Doesn't mean they can't."

She gives me a look. "When's the last time everything came together like that for you or someone you know?"

"Tonight's coming together. In a weird, unexpected way."

"You know what I mean. Something big, like everything working out in the end in some huge, life-changing way." She stares at me expectantly.

I don't need to think about this. I know my answer. "Just because they haven't yet doesn't mean they won't. As long as there's more to the story, there's always hope, right?"

Callie has an odd expression on her face. I don't know her

well enough to understand it. She turns her eyes toward the ground. Finally she says, "I suppose so."

We stand there in silence for a bit until it becomes clear the night is over.

"I should probably go," I say.

Callie walks me out and watches me put on my helmet, which makes me fumble around with the strap a bit more than I usually do. It takes me three times to actually start the bike. She waves good-bye as I pull away.

On the way home, the streets seem more alive than usual. The dark outlines of trees and parked cars are more vivid, pulsating with life. Everything is more than it was just hours ago. And even though I'm only going the maximum thirty-five miles per hour, I feel like I'm flying.

WE HAVE LOST EVEN

When I get home, Dad's reading on the couch.

"How'd it go?" he asks. He puts his book down and takes off his glasses as if to see me better.

"Good."

"Did you get a lot of work done?"

Work? Oh, right. It hadn't felt like work at all. "Yes."

He stares at me for a few moments before dropping his gaze. "Glad we could have this titillating conversation."

"Sure thing," I say, and head upstairs to my room.

Instead of sleeping, I draw Callie. She makes a good subject because of her strong profile. I noticed it while we were on the couch. It's funny how I never noticed in class.

I start with an outline of her face. Then I try to fill in the details, but I can't. They're fuzzy. Does she have freckles? Does her nose curve down at the end, or up? Is her mouth small or wide? Her eyes give me trouble too. I remember their color, like sand, but I can't see them clearly enough. I can manage the pupil okay, but the iris is off and so is the shape. I rip the paper out of my notebook, crumple it up, and toss it to the floor. I start over again on a clean page.

Many pages and disappointing eyes later, I take a break to get a snack. It's late, but the light is still on down in the living room. From the top of the stairs, I see Dad sitting on the couch below. He's hunched over and his hand is on his temple like he's got a headache. I'm about to call out and ask if he's okay, but his voice cuts me off.

"You can't just show up or call me like this," he says.

I duck at the top of the stairs.

"We've been through this. I can't be that person for you anymore. I'm sorry."

His voice is a rough whisper traveling up the stairs to me. It scrapes my gut like sandpaper.

"Leslie. I . . . we are never going to be that."

I listen intently. *Who's Leslie?*

"At one time, yes, but . . . I *do* care about you . . ."

His words are broken up, punctuated with something I can't hear on the other end.

"I have a family. You knew that from the beginning."

Dad stands up and paces a little, listening to this person he says he cares about. Some person I don't know.

"You will get through this, I promise. But I can't be the one to help you through it, I'm sorry. I'm sorry for a lot of things. And I know you're angry and hurt, but please . . . don't call me again."

He ends the call and stares at the phone in his hand.

I move to stand. I don't know what I've just heard, but I know I can't stay here a second longer.

Dad's head snaps up and he sees me.

"Neruda?" He coats my name with the same raspy whisper he used on the phone.

I bolt toward my room. I close the door and lean against it for a few minutes, unmoving. There's no knock from Dad, no attempt to explain what I overheard. I sink down in a lump on the floor, hugging my knees to my chest and replaying Dad's conversation over and over in my mind. It becomes a loop I can't stop hearing. But maybe it's nothing. Maybe I'm jumping to conclusions. All I really know is that he was talking to a woman named Leslie. Leslie could be anyone. Maybe she's a coworker from USC. She could be some long-lost relative for all I know.

Then the floor creaks on the other side of my door. Someone is just outside.

"Neruda?" Dad whispers my name.

I remain silent, still, hoping he will go away.

The floor creaks again. Footsteps travel down the hall to my parents' room. The door opens and closes softly.

Callie's distorted eyes stare up at me from their place on the floor. They look crude and ugly, but I stare at them anyway, willing them to help me block out what's on the other side of the door. Instead, they speak of things I don't want to hear.

I'M EXPLAINING
A FEW THINGS

"Morning, Neruda," Mom says to me when I enter the kitchen. She's sitting at the table, drinking coffee. Everything seems perfectly fine and normal.

I head for the cabinet and find a PowerBar. I want to get out of there quickly.

Dad stops me. "Can I make you some breakfast?" he asks, which is a surefire indication that everything is not fine. Dad hasn't fixed me breakfast since I was, like, ten years old.

"No, thanks," I mumble. I rip open the PowerBar and take a huge bite.

"What about you, love? You want an omelet?"

"I'm okay. That's a sweet offer, babe." Mom places her hand on his. "What're your plans this morning?" she asks me.

"Taking the bus to Ezra's." I stare at my parents' hands and wonder for the millionth time since last night who Leslie is.

"Be careful," Mom says.

I catch Dad's eyes for the first time that morning. That's when I see it. A flash of guilt before he drops his gaze.

"It's just a bus ride," I say.

I push open the screen door and let it slam behind me.

No one comes to the door, no matter how hard I knock at the metal screen. My raps aren't loud enough to be heard over the Latin pop emanating from inside, but I wait, not feeling comfortable enough to enter without being invited in.

Eventually a woman with long black-and-gray wavy hair and a flowered apron comes to the door.

"Hi. Is Ezra here?" I say.

She opens the screen door. "You must be Neruda."

"Yes."

"I'm Cecilia, Ezra's mom."

I can see the resemblance. She's got his eyes and mouth, especially when she smiles.

"Nice to meet you," I say.

"Come on in." She holds the door open for me. "Everyone's out back."

I follow Cecilia through the house and out the sliding glass door to the backyard. A large rectangular table covered by a white tablecloth, plates of food, and purple flowers takes up the middle of the lawn. Seated at the table are a bunch of adults of varying ages. Two little kids are playing on the swing set in the back corner. There's a Ping-Pong table set up on the patio. My stomach reminds me that I've only eaten a PowerBar today when it smells the meat cooking on the grill. I hold my hand against it as if that can stop the growling.

"Neruda!" Ezra sees me and calls out.

"Hey, Ezra." I go up to him and he gives me a hug. Then he grips my shoulder and finds my eyes. "Glad you could make it."

He tilts up the round-rimmed black hat he's wearing.

"Mom, come here and meet my friend Neruda."

She smiles at me and says, "We just met." Then she pulls me in for a hug and whispers in my ear, "Thank you for keeping my boy company while he was in that terrible place."

Her hair smells like shampoo. She pulls away but still holds on to one of my arms. I kind of want her to let go.

"He needs a plate of food, Ezra," she says.

"On it."

"You want something to drink?" she asks. "A beer? No, what am I saying, a soda?"

"Sure," I say. I'm not used to being treated like I'm someone important. Cecilia finally lets go of me and walks over to the table to see if anyone else needs anything.

Ezra makes me two carne asada tacos and one with *pastor* and we sit down together. He introduces me to his whole family: two aunts and uncles, three cousins, his sister and her husband, and his niece and nephew. I greet the men with handshakes and the women with hugs. The only people missing are Ezra's dad, who died a couple of years ago, and his brother, who also passed.

Ezra's mom stands up and addresses all of us. "Today is a good day." She places her hand on Ezra's shoulder. "This is the first birthday in a long time that we get to celebrate at home with you. I am proud of you, son. Those years were not wasted. They happened. They helped shape who you've become, but they do not define you. I look forward to seeing what the future brings. Happy birthday, Ezra."

Cecilia bows her head, as do the others around the table. "Lord, bless this food. Bless this time together. Thank you for family and friends. Amen."

We all say "amen" in response.

"Now eat, before it gets cold," his mom says.

I do as I'm told and close my eyes, savoring the first bite. The carne is just as good as you'd find at the street cart up by me. Ezra's uncle passes me some beans and rice. I add a generous amount of salsa, guacamole, and chips to my plate.

Around the table, Ezra's relatives share all kinds of stories about his childhood.

"What about the time he got all mad and ran away?" his sister says.

"Was that when he broke Nana's dish?" his mom asks.

"Ma—" Ezra starts to say.

"Oh, boy. I was so mad," his mom says.

"You told me that Dad was going to 'handle me' when he got home! Of course I ran away. Packed a bag and rode my bike over to the park."

His aunt Becky says, "Yes, and then you showed up at my house. Oh my goodness. You looked so scared and dejected, *pobrecito*." Poor thing. She reaches out to touch Ezra's cheek. "*Mijo*, I didn't have the heart to turn you in right away. I think I made you a quesadilla and let you watch TV."

"The best quesadilla I'd ever tasted, to this day," Ezra says. "How long was I gone?"

"About four hours," his mom says, and laughs.

"Nah. I remember it feeling like forever."

"So I called Miguel," Aunt Becky says, "and he came to get you."

"You ratted me out," Ezra says, shaking his head at her.

"And he didn't even get a spanking," Ezra's sister says, still sounding bitter even though this happened years ago.

"Nope. Dad took me out for hot chocolate. I remember it

was late and he said he wanted to talk to me, man-to-man. He asked why I'd want to hurt my family by running away. He told me that whatever happens, no matter what bad things we do, there's always a way back through family. Family will be there when everything else is stripped away. You don't turn your back on family."

This last line resonates. The group becomes quiet the way people sometimes do when they have heard something meaningful and need to allow it time to sink in. I can't help but think about my dad.

"And then he grounded me for two weeks the second we got home," Ezra says.

Everyone laughs, dispersing the wave of emotion just as quickly as it settled. They continue to weave in and out of the past. Every time they creep toward the present, the gap of time punctuated by Ezra's absence is awkwardly felt.

Several tacos and sodas later, I go inside to use the restroom and walk past an open door. I know I shouldn't snoop, but it's open, so I figure I can take a look around. The room is clean—too clean—more like a guest bedroom than one actually being used. Dodgers posters and paraphernalia mark the walls, along with a couple of pictures of old, classic cars. A black suitcase sits next to a twin bed. There's a large bookcase filled with mostly comics, stacked. As I walk over to the shelf, I spy a small basket with a pile of pictures inside. I reach for the photos. They're all of a younger Ezra.

"Mom left it exactly the same." Ezra's voice comes from the doorway.

I drop the photo I'm holding of Ezra and a girl at what looks like a school dance.

"I told her she shouldn't. She could have changed it. Made it an office or a guest room or something. She said, 'Why would I do that when you'll be back?'"

"It's a nice room."

"It's a boy's room," Ezra says. He stands with his hands in his pockets and looks around.

I pick up the picture again. "Who's this?" I ask.

It's one of those photos where the guy is standing behind a girl with his arms wrapped around her waist. She's wearing a strapless purple dress. Her black hair falls super long over one shoulder.

"Daisy Torres," Ezra says, his voice heavy with the memory.

"Was she your girlfriend?"

"Yes."

"She's pretty."

"She was gorgeous." He sits on the bed. "We were so young. She was . . . everything. The love of my life. I thought I'd marry her someday. But you know, one mistake, and then"—he snaps his fingers—"ten years pass, and . . . well . . ." Ezra says everything with just enough feeling that I know he still cares for her.

"Where is she now?"

"I don't know. She went to college in Santa Barbara, that's the last I heard. She wanted to be a teacher."

"You didn't stay in touch?"

"What—and date her from prison? Come on, man. She needed to live her life. I didn't want to stop her from doing that."

Two young lovers ripped apart by one misstep. It's tragic, but it gets me thinking.

"So she might still be available," I say.

"What?"

"Well, if you don't know where Daisy is or what she's up to, think of what else you don't know. What if she's single and hoping you will call her?"

"Oh, are you some matchmaker now?"

"I'm just saying, if you still have feelings for her, maybe you should consider looking her up."

Ezra takes the photo from my hand.

"I used to have this picture where she was looking off to the side. I looked at it all the time when I was locked up, until I realized that it wasn't really her anymore, you know? Five years had passed. I had changed. Not only physically but, you know, I'd grown up. And the photo I was looking at was of this beautiful eighteen-year-old girl. But she wasn't a girl anymore. She wasn't *my* girl. And all these experiences that I wasn't a part of now defined her. So I tore up the photo."

He places the picture of them at the dance back in the basket.

"You really never talked to her after you went to prison?"

He shrugs. "She tried to contact me a couple of times, but I didn't want to see her."

"Why?"

"She needed to move on. I knew there was no way I'd be getting out early. And I didn't want to hold her back. So I had to let her go."

"You still love her?" I ask.

Ezra gives me a look, then quickly turns away. "I haven't seen her in ten years. I don't even know her." He puts the basket of photos back on the shelf.

"Santa Barbara's not far. It's only a couple hours away. If she's there, she's practically local," I say.

Ezra stares at me like I've said something he's thought of doing, but then his eyes harden. "No, she's . . . We were a long time ago. It's all good, man—time for me to focus on the future, anyway. Hey, did I tell you I've got an interview set up?"

"That's awesome. For what?"

"A marketing company up in Bakersfield."

"Oh, wow. That's really far. But cool." I try to make my voice sound upbeat, but I don't want Ezra leaving for Bakersfield. He's only been out of prison for six months. I've just gotten used to being able to see him as much as I want. If he moves to Bakersfield, it would be like he is still in prison.

"Yeah, I need to go where I can get a job. A real job. Man, it'll be better than working in my uncle's garage."

"I thought you liked working on cars."

"It's good for now, while I get back on my feet, but it's not what I want to do for the rest of my life."

"Well, then I hope it works out," I say.

"Thanks."

Ezra sifts through the photos in the basket. "Man, if I could go back and talk to my younger self. The things I would tell him . . ."

Instead of the words, he offers a sad smile and points his finger at me. "You ever do anything stupid, I'll kick your ass myself."

I shove my hands in my pockets and grin.

"So what's going on? I can tell there's something bothering you."

I tell him about the conversation I overheard my dad having with Leslie.

"I don't know what to do," I say.

"Well, I think you have two choices: Ignore it and hope that things'll take care of themselves. Or confront him and see what he has to say. But I'll tell you, man, secrets are insidious things. The truth wants to be found out. At least that's my experience."

I hang my head. Suddenly it all feels unbearably heavy.

"Listen," he says, "you're in a tough position, but you don't have all the facts. It could be just some big misunderstanding. If I were you, I wouldn't say anything to your mom just yet. You don't want to hurt her unnecessarily." He puts his hand on my shoulder and squeezes. "Sorry, man, that's a lot to handle."

And now it feels like there's something in the back of my brain that wasn't there before. Some bug burrowing—irritating and present.

"Yeah, it's okay," I say, as if maybe just saying the words will make it so. Maybe if I ignore it, it'll go away.

"Well, I'm here if you need to talk."

"Thanks." That's the cool thing about Ezra. We can talk like that and it's not weird. We don't have to play video games. He doesn't ever make me feel stupid for bringing something up. He's the only person, besides Greyson, I can say anything to without worrying he will freak out or get offended. And he tells me things too. We've got each other's back.

"By the way." He gets up and hands me a book, *Residence on Earth*, by The Poet. "I just started this. Have you read it?"

"Some of it."

Ezra says, "It's good. Here, check this one out." He turns to a page marked with a small yellow sticky tab and reads one out loud called "Walking Around." It's about this man who is angry and tired of being a man, tired of simply surviving, wanting his life to mean something.

"It's powerful," I say, making a note to look up and read the poem again later. *Residence on Earth* is considered the best of The Poet's later works. I find it a little too heavy and depressing, though, because it's about death and how everything is decaying.

Ezra closes the book and puts it back. "I never thought I'd be so into poetry. If they had taught Neruda in school, I probably would have paid more attention."

"Yeah, I know what you mean." They still don't teach him, at least not in any classes I've had.

"How's your art coming along?" he asks.

I show him my sketchbook. He comes to the end, where there are a couple attempts at Callie's eyes.

"Who's this?"

"Just some girl from school. We're partners on a research project."

Ezra nods. "So what's next?"

"What do you mean, what's next?"

"With the girl. The one who's a season."

"Oh, Autumn." I sigh. "I gave her *Twenty Love Songs*."

He whistles. "That was ballsy."

"Yeah, well, it didn't go as planned. She pretty much said she doesn't like me like that." Or probably at all.

"So you're out?"

I shrug. "I don't know." Truthfully, I don't know how to

proceed with her. At this point, I would usually just add her to the list—number eight. My heart feels a little heavy at the thought.

"Girls worth pursuing always take work. I asked Daisy out four times before she finally agreed to hang out with me. How many times have you asked Autumn out?"

"Technically I haven't gotten that far. To the asking-out part."

Ezra laughs. "Oh, man, you haven't even given this your best shot."

"Well, what would you do?"

"I'd start by actually getting to know her. What does she like?"

I try and think about what I know about Autumn, and it's embarrassingly shallow. The point is I want to get to know her better. Isn't that the point of dating?

"I think she plays clarinet."

"Maybe you could ask her to a concert. Or you could draw her something. How many guys does she know who can draw like you? Play up your strengths. She'll be impressed."

"I'm not very impressive when it comes to girls."

"You only need to be to one."

I think about this for a moment. He has a point. "Maybe," I say.

"Go for it. Women are attracted to confidence in a man."

"Autumn's not the kind of girl that you just ask out. She's beautiful." And perfect. Like a painting.

"Look, Neruda, if you want, wait for her to give you a sign. A little nudge of encouragement that she's into you too. Like maybe she waits for you after class. Or maybe a friend of hers comes up to you and says something. Maybe it's a smile. Whatever. You'll know it when you see it. But, man, when you see it, you've got to take it. You're young, what have you got to lose?"

When older people say that, I think they mean it to sound encouraging. But how can it be when some risks feel so big that the very act of taking them feels like you might lose everything?

"Oh, I don't know—just two more embarrassing years left at school, running into her at random moments, feeling completely demoralized by her rejection."

"Possibly," Ezra says. "Or maybe she'll turn out to be the greatest love of your life."

I brighten a little, considering that.

"Don't play it safe. Taking risks is not for the faint of heart."

"Yeah," I say. But I'm still not sure how to handle the whole thing.

"I'll make you a deal," he says. "If you talk to Autumn, really put yourself out there, I'll think about contacting Daisy."

"You will?"

"Yeah," he says.

We shake on it.

Who knows? Maybe there's something to be said for a little persistence.

On the bus ride home, I get a text from Callie.

Did you ever have a recurring nightmare as a child?

I text her back, No, but I dream of chile sometimes.

I've never been, but I feel like I know it through Papi's stories and The Poet. In his poetry, the descriptions are so vivid. I've been to the forest and the beaches he writes about many times in my imagination.

You mean chili? The food?

No, the country.

Oh, haha cool

She doesn't say anything more, but I've got a forty-minute bus ride left, so I send her a text to keep the conversation going.

What about you?

Sometimes, I'm lost in a department store. I'm stuck in the clothes hanging on the rack. I can't get out.

Scary, I type.

Yeah

A text comes in from Dad: Chinese takeout okay for dinner tonight?

I don't answer him. I spend the rest of the ride home typing and deleting snarky responses, thinking about Dad and trying to remember if he's been acting strange. If there have been details that I haven't paid attention to. Any signs I might have missed.

But I've got nothing.

If Dad is cheating on Mom, he's been a pro at it.

It makes me feel sick.

I get off the bus early, giving myself a farther walk home than usual. Something to help clear my head.

As I'm heading up the driveway, Dad calls out, "Hey, Neruda, want to shoot some hoops?"

"No, thanks," I say. "I'm tired."

I brush past him and keep my head down.

Dad's not the only one capable of lying.

THE MORNING IS FULL

The next morning, Mom and Dad plan to go out to breakfast and hit up a farmers' market. She wants me to join them. Instead, I pull the I've-got-tons-of-homework-and-I-really-want-to-do-a-better-job-in-school card. I rarely use it, so when I do, it works very well. Mom sees it as a sign that I'm taking responsibility. Dad doesn't even press me to go like he normally would. Another sign of his guilt.

When they leave, I head right for his office. Dad's laptop sits on top of his desk. His Gmail is already open. It takes me two seconds to type in the name *Leslie* and a slew of emails from someone named Leslie de Prieto pop up. I start with the most recent. A thank-you email for a job recommendation he provided for a position at the USC library. I scroll through the list. They're all dated from last year.

The old picture of Papi and The Poet on Dad's desk unnerves me. It's like they're watching, judging. I turn the picture facedown. They don't need to see this.

I scroll and find a few emails about some mythology class Dad taught. From what I can tell, she was the corresponding TA.

The emails are chatty and friendly, but not romantic or anything incriminating. Then I stumble upon one with the subject "Re: PS." It's a love poem, and I recognize it instantly. Dad's hijacked the words of The Poet, claiming them as his own, giving them to Leslie, twisting them into something dark and ugly.

I spin around in his chair, wondering if he's got anything else on Leslie tucked away.

Dad's a meticulous keeper of all things paper. I scour the books and files and folders on his desk. I open one of the drawers. Inside are his most recent class files, dated and color-coded.

I sift through the papers—some are his notes and assignments, some are student papers. Why he keeps a hard copy of everything is a mystery to me.

I comb through file after file until I finally come across a purple folder from last year's mythology and literature course. And then I see it.

On the class roster is the name Leslie de Prieto, circled and highlighted in yellow, with *TA* next to it.

Her contact information is on another page. Quickly, without really thinking about it, I call the number.

After three rings, a female voice answers. "Hello?"

The voice is soft and a little breathy, as if she had to run to answer the phone. The voice is real and steals my own. I'm mute. I have no idea why I called or what I should say.

"Hello?" she asks again.

I open my mouth, but no sounds come out. Then there's an irritated sigh and a sharper "Hello?" followed by a click.

I stare at Leslie's name on the paper for a moment, then take a picture of her information with my phone and leave the folder on top of Dad's desk.

ODE TO BROKEN THINGS

After a pretty crappy night's sleep, the last thing I want to do is sit in class after class all day long, so I'm actually happy when Mr. Nelson tells us we're going to be doing something different, something to "build a sense of community."

"High school is hard," he says. "You should all have each other's backs."

We give him a collective stare, not even an eye roll.

"Today we're going to play Ultimate Frisbee. And tomorrow, you'll have a writing assignment based on your experiences."

Even though there will be writing involved, I don't care. Anything to get me moving and to forget about my dad and the female voice on the other end of the phone sounds good to me.

When we get on the football field, Mr. Nelson divides us up into two teams. The other team scores on us in the first three minutes, so it's a little stacked in their favor, but I don't care. I just want to play.

When my team has possession, I race past Josh until I'm open, and call out to Traden. He passes me the Frisbee. I catch it and stumble two steps forward. I spy Callie up the line. She's motioning for the disc, so I toss it to her. She catches the Frisbee and quickly tosses it to Hector in the goal. He catches it.

"Yes!" Callie yells. "Great catch, Hector!"

We stand in a line by our goal and wait for Luis's team to be ready to receive our throw. Hector throws it, and Josh tries to catch, but misses. We lose possession.

"Man up!" Callie calls out.

Somehow she has become our team leader and we have accepted this. She commands us and we say "yes, sir." No one challenges her out of fear. That or lack of interest. Regardless, she's clearly in charge, and we would steadily follow her into battle.

In some sick twist from the gods, I stand guard against Luis. Even though he's Mr. Wrestler, I'm actually faster. He tries to get open, but I'm there with him stride for stride.

Manny passes him the disc, and I jump forward to catch it with one hand, then pivot and toss it back to Callie.

Luis swears loudly, and I smile. Just because I'm an artist doesn't mean I'm not good on my feet.

Manny covers Callie. She keeps bobbing in and out, but Manny is bigger. She can't get a clear opening, so I run up and she tosses toward me, but Luis sweeps in and takes possession. He looks down the field to where Josh is wide open and lets the Frisbee fly. I speed after Josh. It's a beautiful throw. The Frisbee sort of hovers in the air before it starts to drop. And even though Josh doesn't have nearly as far to travel, he still can't beat me to the disc. I dive and catch it before I hit the ground.

"It's still in play. Still in play!" Mr. Nelson yells above the cheers of my teammates.

I see Emmy in the goal and toss her the disc. She catches it and we score.

In the end, my team loses by a point. The other team cheers and does a group dance. Someone starts belting out "We Are the Champions" by Queen.

I kick at the tufts of grass and start walking back to class, shoulders a little drooped with defeat. I'm all sweaty and my jeans have a huge grass stain up the side.

Callie heads my way. She looks just as sweaty as I feel. I expect her to walk past me, but she falls into step alongside me instead.

"Guess I'll have to add Ultimate to the skill section of my essay on you," she says.

"What?"

"That play. Where you caught it as you were diving? Impressive."

I keep my eyes on the ground, a bit shy from her praise. Luis knocks into me, which makes me bump into Callie, but before I can say anything, he and Josh are racing ahead like a couple of idiots.

"Nice game," Luis calls over his shoulder.

"Bastard," I mutter just as Callie says, "Jerk." We laugh.

"Rough day?" she asks me.

"No, why?"

"You seem distant. More quiet or something."

"I've just got a lot on my mind."

"Yeah, me too."

I keep trying not to think about it, but it's hard not to replay Leslie's "Hello?" over and over in my mind. She sounded young and she has some kind of an accent. Maybe Southern.

Ezra said I have two choices. But neither of them sound like a good idea. Telling Mom is out of the question. At least, not until I talk to my dad and find out what's really going on first. But acting like I don't know about Leslie, pretending like everything's cool . . . I don't know if I can do that.

"Oh, really?" Callie says. "What do you have going on, Callie? It's so nice of you to ask, Neruda. There's the usual volleyball practices, but I've also got homework—an endless, torturous supply. Plus I have a research project for Art History where I'm supposed to go to some museum and take notes on every Picasso piece that is there."

The name Picasso brings me out of my head. "Sorry," I say. "I'm just . . . distracted. Which museum?"

"I don't know."

"The LACMA has a good selection. You could try there."

"Is that the one with the yellow hanging things?"

She's referring to an art installation piece that you can interact with once you're inside the museum. Thousands of yellow rubbery strings hang down and you can walk through them. It's iconic to the museum and little kids love to run in and out of them.

"You've never been to the LACMA before?" I ask.

"I think I was there once, on a field trip in elementary school," she says. "Not sure."

"I go all the time. We could go together if you want," I offer.

"When?"

"When is the assignment due?"

"Can you do Saturday?" she asks.

"Sure."

I don't know exactly how it happened, but sometime

between Friday night and now, Callie and I have become people who speak to each other. Sort of like friends.

She glances at her reflection as we pass a classroom window.

"Crap. Look at my face! I'm a mess." She laughs and wipes underneath her eyes with the bottom of her shirt. Some of her purple and black makeup now stain it.

"I don't think it looks bad," I say. She's still got some smudges around the sides of her eyes, and the tops of her lids are a faint purple, but it looks nice. Her eyes are brighter and her cheeks are red, still flushed from the game. "Were you going for that model you showed me on Friday?"

"Yeah, but a more toned-down version."

I nod. "You almost got it."

"I'm surprised you noticed," she says.

"I try to be observant."

"Ha."

"It's true. I had an art teacher a couple of years ago who said you never know where you'll get inspiration, so we should always have our feelers out, looking for our next piece. It's why I carry my sketchbook with me all the time."

"Hmm. Maybe I should start carrying one around. You know, to jot down ideas for what I do."

We enter the classroom and grab our bags. "That would be cool," I say.

The bell rings.

"See you later," Callie says.

"Later." I watch her walk away from me, and for the first time, I notice the muscle tone in the back of her legs.

Luis appears next to me and makes a disgusting kissing sound in my ear.

"Someone's got it for Caaallieee," he singsongs.

I give him the finger and walk out of class.

MY AFFLICTED HOURS

I'm excited about my plans to go to LACMA this weekend, so with a burst of energy and confidence, I decide to take Ezra's advice and try again with Autumn. He's right. I shouldn't give up so easily. Autumn Cho is a girl worth fighting for. I find her outside the band room with a friend. While I stand behind a nearby tree and run some possible lines of practice conversation with her in my head, a guy with a guitar case walks up and casually drapes his arm over Autumn's shoulders. She looks up at him and smiles. He keeps his arm on her the whole time they talk.

It's a small gesture, but right now it's too much.

I turn away from them and lean my head against the tree. Then I push off, scraping my arm, but the pain lands much deeper.

Later, in art class, I head right to my desk, and after a quick nod to Greyson, I put my earbuds in and get right to work on my mural design. I need something to distract me from what I just witnessed at lunch.

I touch the sore spot on my arm. It'll be just a faint red line by tomorrow. It won't even leave a scar.

I try to shake the gnawing thought that I would've killed for Autumn to smile at me like that, and begin sketching. I'm actually really thankful for this mural project. It's the one thing I feel like I'm in control of. It's going to be amazing and my first real chance to establish a name for myself as an artist. Plus it'll be my legacy, a gift to the school that'll be up for years.

At the end of class, Greyson comes over.

"Hey, if you need my help when you're painting the wall, let me know," he says.

"Yeah, sure." But I don't think I'll ask him, even though I know he'd do a great job. I need this to be my own thing.

"Gotta go to practice. See you later."

Greyson leaves and I sit there, waiting for Mr. Fisher. He's offered to check out some murals with me to help with the inspiration for the school project. I already have an idea of what

I'm going to do, but I'm looking forward to seeing some stuff around town. LA is awesome in that it has over fifteen hundred "official" murals, not to mention loads more that are undocumented. There are two whole alleys of them over by the old, cheap movie theater near my house.

The alley has everything from alien-looking one-eyed creatures, to a gangster king holding court, to some kind of Aztec flying deity, to yellow and green shapes running down a concrete wall and into the asphalt. On the side wall of the theater is a huge Jesus in his typical white robe, with long brown hair and his hands held open in front of him. Around the corner from Jesus, multicolored street art and gang signatures fill a whole side of the building and brick wall. The wall changes periodically, with new art pieces replacing the older ones. The graphic style isn't really my thing, but I do love the creepy ghost girl with long blue hair, no eyes or nose, and only stitches where her mouth should be.

It's cool to be surrounded by so much art. It's better than looking at old, dirty buildings. And new murals pop up all the time.

As I'm waiting for Mr. Fisher, Luis enters the classroom. "What up, lover boy," he says.

He sits on top of a desk and starts messing around on his phone. *What's he doing here?* I ignore him. Seeing Luis once today was more than enough.

"Oh, good. You're both here. Do you boys know each other?" Mr. Fisher asks when he emerges from the back room.

I look at Luis and he says, "Yeah, we know each other."

"Great," Mr. Fisher says. "We'll stay local. Ready to go?"

I don't get it. "Both of us?" I ask.

"Luis is going to join you on the mural project." Mr. Fisher begins searching his pockets, rummaging through the drawers in his desk.

Luis? Boob-drawing, penis-drawing Luis? A heat moves up my neck. I try to keep calm. There's no way he's going to touch my mural.

"Um, Mr. Fisher, can I have a word?"

"Sure." He locates his keys and grabs a folder from the top of his desk. "Can we walk and talk?"

"In private?"

I don't wait for him to answer. I head for the back room, where he keeps all the art supplies.

"Is something wrong?" Mr. Fisher asks.

"I thought I was the one working on the mural."

"You are, and you will still run point on it, but I've asked Luis to work on it too."

"Why?"

"Because it'll be good for him, and good for the mural to represent multiple artistic viewpoints. Luis has some real potential."

Yeah, the potential to ruin everything.

"Not from what I've seen," I say.

Mr. Fisher puts on his brown beanie. "Luis is in my intro class, so I've seen some of his work. I think it would be nice for him to partner with you on this. It will be good for him to learn from you and to be a part of something inspiring. Besides, his parents just gave a generous donation to the school, so this will count toward both of your community service hours."

It all becomes clear.

"Can't he volunteer to do something else?"

"Neruda, this will be good for both of you."

"Mr. Fisher, Luis and I . . ." But I don't know how to describe my relationship with Luis because I can't stand him. "We have history," I say, "and it isn't a good one."

"Well, this'll be your chance to write a new history, then."

"But he's . . ."

"Neruda, every great artist eventually needs an apprentice. Think of Luis as yours."

"Shouldn't I get to choose my apprentice?"

Mr. Fisher sighs. "You're still heading up the project, Neruda. Luis can't compete with your ability. I expect that he will mainly assist you, and maybe you can show him a few techniques along the way."

I glance at Luis. He's drawing boobs on the whiteboard.

"Listen, we're on a tight deadline now because we need the

mural ready for the opening of the new wing in the library, so you might appreciate the extra hand."

Doubtful.

"Look." Mr. Fisher places his hand on my shoulder. "Think of this as something you're doing as a favor to me, for the good of the school. And I'll look for opportunities to give you a solo project or two in the future. Ones that'll be excellent for your portfolio."

I raise my eyebrows, curious about what kind of projects he has in mind.

"You're my top student and I wouldn't be asking you to do this if I didn't think you could handle it."

Praise followed by guilt. A classic teacher and parent move.

As Papi used to say, *"Si quieres el perro, acepta las pulgas."* If you want the dog, accept the fleas. The problem is, I don't want the dog.

Mr. Fisher frees my shoulder and pats me on the back. "This will be a good experience, or at least a learning one. Now, let's go. We have a few stops to make."

I don't even try to hide my dejection when I follow him out. Luis grins at me and falls into step alongside Mr. Fisher.

This cannot be happening.

AND HOW LONG?

Luis rides shotgun in Mr. Fisher's car. He doesn't even ask me. He assumes he has earned the spot. I stare out the window in the back, fuming. Mr. Fisher turns on some music, a Latin hip-hop song. At least we don't have to talk to each other.

"Ozomatli," Luis says.

"Yeah. These guys are the best. I used to see their live shows all the time."

"Cool."

I'm seething in the back, irritated about their bonding over music. And I'm pissed that Mr. Fisher is forcing me into this collaboration. Just when I thought life couldn't suck any more.

Our first stop isn't far away—a mural at a small public library. It's not actually on the wall, but on two large panels that have been mounted to the wall.

"Is this oil?" I ask.

"Yep."

"You want me to do *this*?" Luis asks, as if he could actually paint something like it. The panels show these two white kids picking flowers and playing with butterflies and birds. It's a good painting, but not something I'm interested in doing either.

"Of course not," Mr. Fisher says. "I just want the two of you to see what's out there and what's possible so you can start brainstorming your own ideas."

I've already started brainstorming *my* ideas. Actually, I've got the whole mural planned out. I don't need Luis's ideas. Or his help.

"This is not really what we're looking for in terms of content, because it's not really a representation of who or what our school is, but it works—it shows kids having fun and it's perfect for a library. What I'd like you to do at every stop is just take some notes about the piece—the form, the medium, the size, and the message you think it's trying to convey."

Luis and I stare at him.

"Go ahead."

I pull out my sketchbook, and Luis opens up a black spiral

notebook. Ha. Amateur. He turns the page and I see a bunch of graffiti lettering. Of course.

After I make notes on the color palette, the style of the portraits, and the perspective of the piece, and Luis takes notes on whatever, we get back in the car. This time, I take the front seat. If Luis is upset about it, he doesn't show it, which is even more annoying. I glance at him in the rearview mirror, but he's looking out the window. This guy is really getting on my nerves.

Next, Mr. Fisher takes us over to my neighborhood—Highland Park. It's a mixture of Mexican grocery markets, barbershops, tattoo parlors, dollar stores, art galleries, pizza joints, yoga and CrossFit centers, and swanky cafés and restaurants with vegan options. Mr. Fisher tells us the majority of murals we're going to look at today are in this part of the city. I wonder if we'll go by the movie theater.

"This area has changed so much," Mr. Fisher says, as if he has to explain it to me. We've lived here for years, long before it became one of the cool, hip neighborhoods in Northeast LA, or NELA. I like the way it's changed; my parents are less on board. The restaurants are better, but everything's more expensive. It's definitely an eclectic neighborhood with artists, educators, mechanics, stylists, musicians, old gang members, housecleaners, and Hollywood industry types all swimming alongside one another.

"I suppose it's progress," he continues, "but I miss the days when you could get lunch for under ten dollars and York Street wasn't a bearded hipster parade. I guess it's better than a street full of car and muffler repair shops, though. There's a huge artist community here, which is why I love it. Have you guys ever gone to Second Saturday?"

"Yes," I say.

"What is it?" asks Luis.

"The second Saturday of every month, artists from the area display their work to the public. It's kind of like the Downtown Art Walk. You guys should check it out."

"I'd be down for that," Luis says.

It's bad enough I have to spend after-school hours with Luis. But a weekend? No, thanks.

Mr. Fisher pulls over and we get out to look at a spray painting called *A Couple of Immigrantes* in a shady-looking alley. It's of two old Mexican men wearing white pants and shirts and big tan hats. There's a tag in the upper right-hand corner that reads MAN ONE—a well-known artist who creates murals all over the world. It's pretty cool to have some of his right here in LA.

We walk a bit and Mr. Fisher shows us another work of Man One's a couple of blocks away, called *Capturing Our Identity*. It's a huge face of a child, again done with aerosol but in different blocks of color, with tagging-style letters along the side. It's large and right in the middle of a neighborhood.

That's the cool thing about murals—they automatically give an environment an artistic identity. And both of these murals are in parts of the city that could use some art against the colorless shades of gray.

When Luis isn't watching, I take a picture of him with my phone and text Callie: Guess who I'm with?

She doesn't respond right away, so when Luis looks at me, I put the phone in my back pocket.

"This next one is by a street artist—Codak. Interested to see what you guys think," Mr. Fisher says.

We drive to a run-down building with black bars on the windows, and Mr. Fisher parks right in front of the mural. He pulls out his phone and begins reading aloud about the piece.

"It's called *Ravens Night and Arising Flight*. You can see the raven here." Mr. Fisher points to what looks like the beak of a bird coming out of different kinds of geometric shapes and curves all swirling together.

Luis stands in front of it for a few moments. Finally he says, "This is awesome."

I don't think it's all that awesome. Not because I don't appreciate the artistry; I do. It's just not me.

"I thought you'd like the street art style of it, Luis."

"For sure." Luis touches the wall and bends to look closer. I can't tell if it's an act or if he's really interested.

He and Mr. Fisher talk through the mural while I stand

off to the side. It's a decent mural and fits the wall and the neighborhood well, but if Mr. Fisher thinks I'm going to suddenly turn into a street artist to help Luis hone his own style, he's wrong.

"You guys up for one more?"

"Yeah, sure," Luis says.

I nod.

I grab the backseat and sink down, sulking. I know that I'm kind of being a baby about it, but I don't care. Luis is a problem I should be facing only in fourth period. He shouldn't be here, now, sitting in the front seat with the window rolled down, looking out and smiling like a happy puppy.

The last mural is along a low concrete wall in a parking lot. As soon as I see it, my heart perks up. It's a collection of portraits done in black and white and in all different styles.

Mr. Fisher reads from his phone again. "This is by a group called Unified Group of Los Angeles Residents, UGLAR for short, and it's a mural series that'll stretch across LA when it's finished."

I touch the forehead of a large old man. The detail is amazing, especially the eyes. I let my fingers run across all the faces, each one distinct, from the ethnicity of the person to the drawing technique. Some are cartoonish and street art in style, but there is also more of what I do too. More realism. I love it. It's perfect. It reinforces my plan for the mural at school and gives me some new ideas.

"This is your thing, right, Neruda?" Luis asks.

"I guess."

He nods to my book. "I've seen your stuff. You could do this."

The compliment throws me. "Maybe."

"Does this inspire some ideas?" Mr. Fisher asks.

"Yeah, definitely," I say.

"Luis, why don't you show Neruda some of your sketches."

Luis actually looks shy when he hands me his book. He shoves his hands in his pockets and studies the wall while I flip through it. They're what I expected. Immature, juvenile, crude lettering, simplistic. Any kid who is trying to copy your basic tagging lettering could do what he's done. I'm about to toss the book back to him when one page catches my attention. It's of a girl with laser beams coming out of her eyes. A lizard is crawling out of her open mouth. Her hands are outstretched and on fire.

"You did this?" I ask him, pointing to the page.

Luis nods.

I stare at the girl before shutting the book. I'm surprised.

We head back to school, Mr. Fisher and Luis chatting about who knows what. I'm lost in thought as ideas for the mural start swirling in my head and trickle down to my hand. I don't stop sketching until Mr. Fisher drops us off by the front entrance.

"Maybe we can talk tomorrow about the direction," he says. "Or better yet, why don't you and Luis talk first and then pitch your idea to me. I have no doubt you'll come up with something artistic and meaningful that the school will love."

Mr. Fisher pulls away and raises his hand in a wave.

"I guess we could meet at my house if you want. Maybe tomorrow after school?" I offer this only so I won't disappoint Mr. Fisher.

"Whatever you say, boss. You're in charge."

If I were really in charge, there's no way I'd be standing here discussing an artistic partnership with Luis.

As soon as Mr. Fisher's car is out of sight, we scatter in opposite directions like two opposing forces.

GENTLEMAN ALONE

Callie calls just as I enter the house.

"Hello?"

"Tell me about Luis!"

I explain my predicament: how I'm now being forced into a mural collaboration with him.

"Are you serious?" she asks.

"Completely."

"Hilarious."

"I'm glad you find humor in my pain."

"It's just . . . No, you're right, it's bad. You should just treat it like a social experiment."

I get the feeling that she can't stand Luis any more than I can, which makes me happy and also curious.

"How come you don't like him?" I ask.

"He's just so . . . base, you know. Like, so on the surface. You know exactly what a guy like Luis is after. I mean, he's cute in that sort of Latino-rebel way. But he's trouble for sure."

I feel a pang of something when she mentions how cute he is. There is nothing redeemable about Luis. But I note too that she seems to like Latinos.

"Can he even draw?" she asks.

"He's got some basic ability."

"That sucks for you, then."

"Why?"

"Because it sounds like you're stuck working with him. Maybe he's got some other surprises in store," she says.

"Yeah, like dismembered heads wrapped in plastic in his basement." I cringe a little because the thought may not be too far from the truth.

"Eww . . . or—and I hate to say this." Callie hesitates. "Maybe he's more decent than we think."

There's a pause as if we're both thinking over what she's said.

"Nah," I say, and we laugh.

"So how was practice?" I ask.

"The usual. Coach had us do sweepers and lunges and bur-
pees. Two people threw up, and I almost did too. He wants us
in extreme physical condition heading into our next game."

The front door opens.

"Neruda?" Dad calls out.

Callie's telling me about the team they'll be playing when I
cut her off. "Sorry, I've got to go."

"Okay, bye," she says.

I hang up and head for the stairs.

"How was school?" Dad asks me just as I reach the bottom
step.

"Fine," I say, and continue going up, holding on to the railing for more than just physical support.

"Neruda?"

I stop but don't turn around.

"Listen, I don't know what you think you overheard the
other night, but everything's fine. Your mom and I are happy.
There's nothing to worry about."

He doesn't say anything about the file I left on his desk. He
doesn't even mention Leslie's name. But I know what I heard,
and I hate him for it.

"Please promise me you won't say anything," he says, fully
admitting his guilt.

I turn around to face him, but he doesn't look me in the
eye. He offers no explanation, no apology for what he's done.

He leaves me there, standing on the middle of the stairs, gripping the wooden rail.

The gall of his request shocks me. I didn't agree to this role. I don't want anything to do with his deception.

My heart speeds up like it sometimes does when I'm uneasy. I feel it fluttering in my chest.

I push off the railing and run to the bathroom. I almost don't make it in time. I throw up more than once and try to ignore the burning in my throat and nose. I lean my head against the cool rim of the toilet seat, hold my chest, and do some breathing exercises until my heart returns to normal and I can't feel it anymore.

ALLIANCE

The next day at lunch, I sit down on the part of the low wall zigzagging across campus that gives me the best view of the quad. I'm sketching the scene before me—groups scattered throughout, clusters of students standing or sitting or passing by. It's crowded. I take notice of the condition of the grass—patchy like a calico cat, mostly brown and dead, with an occasional swath of green. The trees are skinny with small, fragile leaves dangling on their branches.

Greyson plops down next to me and starts eating a sandwich.

He points to Jasmine. She's standing with some of the other

foreign exchange students. "You think she's seeing the guy from Finland?"

"I don't know."

"It's probably the accent," he says, his mouth full. "Girls like guys with accents."

"That would mean she'd like every guy here, since to her, Americans have the accent."

"Good point," he says.

I look around.

"Where's Mercy?" I ask.

"We broke up."

I glance at him sideways. "Sorry."

"It's all right. Wasn't meant to be."

I wait for him to say more, but he doesn't seem that broken up about it. I shouldn't be surprised, considering he told me earlier that's what he was thinking.

"How'd she take it?"

"She cried." He watches Jasmine. "I hate it when they cry." He shifts his attention to my drawing. "I can't believe Fisher put Luis on the mural and not me. What was he thinking?"

"Maybe you should have your parents donate money."

"Can Luis even draw?" he asks.

"Doesn't matter."

"So, what're you going to do?" Greyson asks.

I shrug. "It's not like Mr. Fisher gave me a choice."

Jasmine breaks from her group, and Greyson stands.

"I've got to go do something."

"Putting in the work?" I tease him with his own phrase.

He grins. "See you later."

He's jogging after Jasmine before I can say good-bye. I watch him fall into step beside her. They're talking and laughing like they're old friends. How does Greyson do that? He makes it look so easy, so smooth. Like it's not any work at all.

At home after school, I dial Leslie de Prieto's number again. I know it's stupid. But if my dad won't talk to me, and I can't talk to my mom, maybe Leslie can give me some answers. Something to explain this whole thing.

"Hello?" she says.

This time she only says it once before hanging up.

Just seconds later, my phone rings. I freeze. Leslie's number pops up on the screen. I'm such an idiot. I should have called her from another line. I let it ring and ring.

While I'm freaking out, my phone vibrates, signaling that I've got a new voice mail.

I'm about to press play when a black Prius pulls up and Luis gets out. I stand up and shove the phone into my back pocket.

"You could've told me you didn't live in South Pas," Luis says when I open the front door.

He walks in and starts wandering around the living room before I've even invited him in. Jerk.

"Is anyone else here?" he asks.

"No," I say. "My parents are at work. I've just got to grab some things from my room first," I say, making it clear that Luis should wait downstairs.

He follows me up and hovers in the doorway.

I get some blank sheets of paper, a ruler, some pencils and erasers. I also grab colored pencils in case we want to play around with a color scheme.

"Are these all yours?" Luis asks of the drawings on my wall.

"Mostly."

He stands in front of a portrait I did of a homeless guy and his shopping cart by the Metro station.

"Huh."

If Luis likes it, he doesn't let on.

"What's on your walls?" I ask, trying to make the best of this crappy situation.

"Trophies. Wrestling posters. A calendar with hot chicks."

Figures. "You're really into wrestling, huh?"

"Yeah. I've been doing it since I was seven. My dad wrestled through college. He even made the US national team before he got injured."

Luis goes over to my desk, where I keep a stack of sketch-books. He grabs one and starts looking through it before I can tell him not to.

"Damn, Neruda. Didn't expect this from you."

He pages through my drawings from a nude class.

"I studied nudes last summer," I tell him.

"You drew these in a class?" He holds up the side profile of a woman's bare torso. "You mean you copied a picture?"

"No, they were live nudes."

"A naked chick just stood there for you to draw her?"

"Basically, yeah."

"Shit. Sign me up for that class. Can I keep this?"

"No." I go to grab the book, but Luis swivels around and moves it out of my reach.

"Hey, I'm not finished looking."

"Just put it back." I drop my hand.

"Okay. Okay. But . . . damn. This is beautiful stuff."

"Look, I don't have all afternoon, so we need to start."

This time I take the book from Luis, set it on my desk, turn off the light, and walk out of my room. He follows me back downstairs to the kitchen table.

"So I was thinking we could draw the quad and the dif-ferent people and things happening." I show him my prelimi-nary sketches of the mural. "Something like this. Basically it's like capturing a scene at lunch." I've drawn quick, almost portrait-like images of who I've seen walking around, sitting, talking.

"I know them." He points to my picture of a guy and girl embracing against a wall.

"Who doesn't?"

They're two sophomores who are more into PDA than any couple in the history of the world. Teachers don't even try to break them apart anymore. And they always make out in the same spot.

"We could do one giant orgy under the sun," Luis says. "And with what I saw upstairs, the detail you could provide . . ."

I give him a look that says *shut it*. "Anyway, I can pull all of this together in one sketch in the next day or two and then we can start on the wall."

"Wait, so that's it?"

"What do you mean?"

"I don't get a say? No offense, but it's kind of boring."

I glare at him. "Boring?"

"Yeah."

"So what are your exciting ideas?"

He opens his notebook and shows me a bunch of skyscrapers, like Downtown LA. He turns the page and there's an octopus wrapping one of its arms around a building.

"What's with the octopus?"

He shrugs. "It's cool."

I'm not sure what I'm supposed to do with that. Besides, this is still my mural project, even though I have to work with him. Mr. Fisher didn't say anything about Luis getting a say in the design. He can paint what I tell him.

"Look, Luis, I'm not sure what Mr. Fisher promised you, but I'm overseeing the project, and I just don't see how an octopus fits."

"It can represent how the school is squeezing the life out of us."

I sigh. "Let's just do a warm-up."

"What's that?"

I stare at him. "Just sketch whatever comes to mind when you picture the quad. Fifteen minutes." Idiot.

I unroll the ream of paper and we work on opposite sides of the table. When we start drawing, the only sound is our pencils.

When time is up, Luis has drawn crude skyscrapers in the corner again, this time with the sunlight shooting through the windows and beaming out toward the quad. The quad is like ours, but it's also more futuristic or something. It's less dirt and trees and more concrete, more urban. I cut out some of the figures I've drawn to show him where they'd go. We step back and take it in.

I'm annoyed to admit it, but it actually looks kind of decent.

"I like all the light," I say. "What if the light is illuminating everything, kind of setting fire and spreading through the whole quad, touching people as it goes?"

"You know how to do that?"

"I could try."

I hear a car pulling into the driveway.

"I think my mom's home."

"Does she know you draw naked chicks?"

I ignore Luis and get up to greet her at the kitchen door.

"Hi, Mom."

She places her briefcase on the counter and grabs a Diet Pepsi from the fridge.

"This is Luis."

"Oh yes, *Luis*." She throws a quizzical glance my way. I can almost see her piecing together that Luis is the guy I got into a fight with.

"Pleasure to meet you, Mrs. Diaz." I roll my eyes as he pretends to be a decent human being.

Mom sees the sketches on the table.

"We're working on the mural," I say. "Mr. Fisher's idea."

She studies our sketch for a minute. "I like it. Very cool city with the lights."

It bugs me that she points out Luis's elements over mine.

"Thanks," he says.

"What about the people?" I ask.

"Yeah, they're good too, a little rough, but you'll fix that."

She leaves the kitchen and heads upstairs. "Nice to meet you, Luis."

"You too," he says. "I gotta go."

"Okay. I'll run this past Mr. Fisher tomorrow," I say, and follow Luis to the door.

"Cool," he says.

I don't watch him leave, but a few seconds later, I hear his car peeling away.

I create a preliminary rough sketch for the mural based on what Luis and I talked about. His comment about my idea being boring still grates on my mind, so I start to research murals online. Most are pretty uninspiring, but I do find something interesting about these art installation walls started by an artist named Candy Chang in New Orleans a few years back. She created the first piece after she lost someone she loved, and the exhibit is like a giant chalkboard with tons of lines that say: *Before I die I want to* . . . People have written what they want to do in the space that follows, and now there are installations up all over the world, from Japan to Canada to Mexico to Australia. But the walls themselves aren't these amazing pieces. It's more about the idea of people—total strangers—creating the piece together that makes it interesting.

Some of the things people write are funny. Someone wrote that he wanted to fight The Rock before he died. Other stuff is much more inspirational, like the people who wrote that they want to abandon all insecurities or that they want to see equality for all people. In Spain, someone wrote that they wanted to be swept up in a passionate love affair.

Some walls have different prompts, but the same open-ended idea. Instead of *Before I die*, one wall says, *When I graduate* . . . There's another that says, *If you knew me* . . . , and one was even started in Pasadena with the prompt *One day I will* . . .

I find mention of a wall in Santiago, Chile, and I'm curious to know what the Chileans put up. The wall is titled *11 de Septiembre* (September 11), but it's not about the terrorist attacks in the United States. It's referring to the bloody military coup of 1973. The event right before Pablo Neruda's death. The prompt for writing is *Yo siento* . . . I feel . . . I try to read some of the inscriptions, but I can't make out the words from the photo. The wall is dense with multicolored writing.

I wonder if we could create something like this at school alongside the mural. It would be a cool form of self-expression and maybe even spark conversations, if people were actually honest.

When I'm finished researching and doing homework, I head downstairs. Dad and Mom are in the kitchen talking and making dinner. Dad's putting noodles in a pot of boiling water.

"Neruda, when do you think you can clean the garage?" he

asks when he sees me. Normally, Dad would just tell me to clean the garage, but he's being all nice about it, as if that will fix things between us. "Can you do it this weekend?"

"Can't. Have a school project." My trip to LACMA isn't necessarily for my assignment, but technically it's for Callie's, so it counts.

"All right, the next weekend, then."

"Fine."

"How was work, honey?" Dad asks Mom. "Did you get that new client?"

Dad's pouring it on thick with Mom, being overly attentive, asking more questions than usual. You'd think she works for the FBI with how he's hanging on every word she says. When he pulls her in for a hug and a kiss, I feel sick.

I tell them I'm going out and don't wait for any protest about how I haven't eaten dinner yet.

"Save me a plate!" I yell over my shoulder, and rush out the door.

I head to Greyson's, but his mom tells me he's at the school volleyball game. I could go back home, but I don't feel ready to face my parents yet. So I get back on my scooter and make my way to school.

When I enter the gym, music is blaring and both teams are already on the court, warming up. I scan the bleachers and spy

Greyson at the top. He's sitting with Jasmine and a couple of the other foreign exchange students. I have to give him credit. He does work fast.

Greyson introduces me to them when I sit down next to him. "Guys, this is Neruda."

They say their names down the line as if in a roll call: Jasmine, Grete, and Peter.

"Grete is from Norway, and Peter is from New Zealand. How cool is that?" Greyson says.

"Pretty cool," I say.

The referee blows a whistle and the first game begins. Things move quickly with sounds of sneakers squeaking on the gym floor, girls calling out plays, and the ball hitting flesh. Callie's at the net. The setter passes her the ball, right on the net, and Callie slams it over. Two of the opposing team jump up to block her on the other side of the net, but the ball makes it through and our team scores its first point. I cheer and even yell, "Go, Callie!"

She smiles and a couple of her teammates give her high fives before she goes back into position at the net. I'd seen the team play last year, so I know how good Callie is, but I don't remember noticing how good she looked while playing.

I keep my eyes on her for the rest of the game.

Greyson, on the other hand, barely watches the game. He and Jasmine talk almost the whole time. From what I can tell,

Grete and Peter are together. The hand-holding is a dead give-away. I am the odd man out.

As usual.

Our team is in the lead going into the last game, and it's looking like we'll take the win until Callie makes a strategic mistake. She misreads a hitter and goes for the block, but her opponent just taps it lightly over to the left. The ball hits the floor and the other team scores. Callie swears and bends over with her hands on her knees. She shakes her head and then pulls herself up.

We end up winning the final game, but it is tight. I contemplate congratulating Callie, but she's standing with a bunch of girls, so I just head out.

Afterward, I go with Greyson and the others to get something to eat. Peter is explaining the difference in New Zealand coffee, but I'm not really listening. I'm thinking about Callie—how great she looked out there, how great she is at volleyball, how great she is, period.

My phone buzzes.

It's a photo of a naked woman with enormous breasts.

Luis.

thought you'd like her

I'm about to turn my phone off when I notice I've got a voice mail.

"Be right back," I tell them.

I get up from the table so I can listen to it.

"I'm not sure who this is, but if you don't stop prank calling me, I'm going to report this number."

Leslie. I completely forgot.

I stand there for a second, numb. Then I press delete.

I LIKE FOR YOU
TO BE STILL

On Saturday morning, I'm halfway up Callie's front steps when her door opens and she walks out in her usual black boots. But she's also got on torn skinny black jeans, a white T-shirt, and a black leather cropped jacket.

"Hey," she says as she struts toward me.

I glance back at my small scooter on the street.

"Did you forget what kind of bike I have? It's not a Harley."

"It's all about perception," she says. "Sometimes you have to feel it, you know." I look at her face. Her eyes sparkle like the ocean when the sun hits it.

She takes the spare helmet I offer and places it on her

head. I get on the bike, and before I can tell Callie what to do, she hops on behind me. She doesn't wrap her arms around my middle, like I would have thought. She holds on to the sides of the seat instead. It's still a small bike, though, so I feel her body lean into mine as I turn left down the road.

I've never had a girl ride with me before. I imagine what it'd be like to ride along the coast or something, going until we are exhausted. Just riding forever, Callie and me. We wouldn't stop unless we needed to, and even then, only in some strange town where we didn't know anyone. This would be the first of our many adventures together, and by the end, we'd be completely in love. Not that I'm into Callie, but it's fun to dream about who my number nine could be.

My fantasy is short-lived because the Metro station is only a couple minutes down the road. We get on and sit across from each other.

"What's in the bag?" she asks, pointing to my backpack.

"Some lunch for later. I figured we'd get hungry, and things are kind of expensive there, so . . ."

"Thanks. That was very thoughtful of you."

I shrug. "Close game Tuesday night," I say, changing the subject.

"You were there?"

"Yeah."

"You saw me miss that play, then."

"Which one?" I ask. I know the play she's talking about, but I don't want her to think I thought it was a big deal.

"The one where I thought she was going to hit it, and so I jumped, but she just tapped it. Oh, man, I felt horrible. I should have anticipated that."

"Yeah, but that didn't lose the game or anything."

"No, but it won them a point. Coach brought it up immediately after the game. He thinks we can win league this year and go on to the CIF finals. So he needs me to try harder."

"You guys are great," I say, then add, "you're great."

"Thanks," she says. "I'm not sure I'm really good enough to continue in college."

"You're good enough," I say, and I wonder if it's normal for Callie to doubt herself.

"Maybe. Not sure if I want to, though."

We're both silent for a moment.

"You do any more of those faces?" I ask.

She smiles wide. "Yeah. Here." She takes out her phone to show me her latest work, something she designed last night. One side of her face is a brown tree trunk, and its branches spread across the other side. "What do you think?"

I give her a thumbs-up because I don't have the language for what she does. It's so beautiful, so inspiring, but saying so feels like it would somehow make her work less magical.

I watch her flip through images on her phone, surprised

at how comfortable it feels to hang out with her like this.

I tell her about my mural tour with Mr. Fisher and my sketching with Luis. Suddenly it's our stop.

As soon as Callie sees the tall gray lampposts that mark the entrance to the Los Angeles County Museum of Art, she exclaims, "Oh, this is cool!"

"I thought you said you'd been here before."

"Yeah, but I don't remember these." She touches one of them, pulls out her phone, and takes a selfie.

I've been coming here since I first started studying art and began learning about the different mediums. One teacher suggested we go often to observe styles and practice copying.

Imitation isn't just flattery. It's also a great way to learn. The harder part is leaving imitation and finding your own voice. When you do that—find your own conviction, your signature—you become a real artist. That can take years. I'm still trying to find mine.

The museum is free for us since we're under eighteen, but we still have to stand in line and get tickets.

Callie picks up a map. "Where should we go first?"

"We can just walk around. There's plenty to see, but I'd start in the Ahmanson Building because that's where the Picassos are."

"Okay. Cool."

We enter the Ahmanson and walk quietly up the thick

marble stairs to the left, through the halls of hanging wall art.

"Are you going to give me a tour or something?" she whispers.

"Um, sure," I say. We stop in front of a couple Picasso portraits. "This one is called *Head of a Woman in Profile*. This is one of Jacqueline, his second wife."

Callie reads the description. "This says the painting represents the perfect Mediterranean woman?" She takes out her phone to snap a picture, but the blue-suited docent standing close by tells her no pictures are allowed.

Callie stands directly in front of the portrait. She tilts her head to one side, then to the other. After a few moments, she says, "Yeah, I don't get it. That's got to be the ugliest woman. Her eyes and lips are all smashed together. He must've hated her."

"Actually, he loved her. She was the only woman he painted for his last seventeen years."

"What a strange way to paint her, then."

"Well, he was a cubist, but this one is from the end of his life. It's more marked by wild expressionism. His blue period is better," I say, though I'm not a huge fan of Picasso either.

"Why?"

"Just my personal preference. It's not as abstract and everything is in a blue hue."

"Hence the name," she says.

"Hence the name. There are some of those paintings in a different area of the museum. We can see those later if you want."

"Okay. I'm going to take some notes on this one."

I look at the other paintings while she types on her phone. The museum is a little crowded today because it's a weekend. I prefer it when it's emptier.

After about ten minutes of note taking, Callie says, "Finished. Sorry."

"Don't be sorry," I tell her. "I could stay here all day."

"I don't know many guys—wait, I don't know *any* guys who would choose to spend the entire day in a museum."

I shrug. I can't tell if she thinks this is a good thing or a bad thing. At the very least, it's something for her to put into her report. "So, you want to go to the other Picassos or do you want to look around?"

"Whatever you think," she says. "You're the expert."

"Well, do you like Monet? There's a large collection here."

"He's the one who did a lot of landscapes and flowers, right?"

"Yeah, you've probably seen his stuff on calendars mostly. Or there's Diego Rivera over at the Art of the Americas Building. You know what, let's go there. There's some paintings I want to show you. Then we can circle back around and check out the other Picassos. There's a drawing of one of his other lovers, at the beginning of his career, that you might want to use for your paper."

Callie smiles at me.

"What?"

"Nothing." She gestures with her hand. "Lead the way."

I show her a couple more pieces in the building, avoiding the floors with the art of the ancient Near East and of the Pacific since I'm not as familiar with those periods, before we head outside and into the art installation that features long plastic yellow tubes hanging from an iron structure.

"*Penetrable*," I tell her.

"What?"

"That's the name of the piece."

"It looks like yellow spaghetti."

Callie stands in the middle of the yellow rubber tubes and it's like she's caught inside a yellow rainfall. I take a picture of her on my phone. Then she grabs some of the yellow strands and makes a serious model pose, followed by a crazy face. I laugh.

"Your turn," she says.

I just stand there.

"Come on," she says. "Do something silly."

As I'm thinking through the poses I can do, trying to find something that would look cool, she says, "Just jump really high."

I jump as high as I can.

She takes my picture. "Awesome, check it out."

She's captured me midair with my face tilted up toward the sky.

"It looks like you're floating," she says, and smiles up at my face.

I smile down at her. She's right. In fact, I kind of feel like I'm floating right now.

We move on to the next building, the one with the American artists.

"I love it here because of all the old oil portraits," I tell her as we walk through the hall. The paintings are huge with large, chunky gold frames. I show Callie the portrait of a woman in a white dress and pearls—*Portrait of Mrs. Carr* by Diego Rivera. "Classic."

"Is that what you want to do someday?" she asks.

"Not that style so much. Oil is a pretty difficult medium. But I love the detail and how the painter felt about her."

"What do you mean? How can you tell how the painter felt about her?"

"Look at the way he uses color and light and shadow . . . the care here." I reach out and run my hand in front of the portrait, illustrating where I'm talking about. "And here."

"Hmm. I don't really see it."

"You will, the more you look. I've just started using oils. It's crazy how different it is from acrylic or watercolor."

"That's cool."

"Yeah, I'm liking it so far."

"So this is what you do in your free time?" she asks.

"Yeah, or I draw."

"What kinds of things do you draw?"

"Sometimes I'll actually draw paintings, if there's some technique I want to learn from the piece. Like if I want to practice shading or something. But I prefer live subjects."

We enter a room with a huge mural. I stop and take it in. Normally, I would have walked right past, but I make a mental note to tell Luis about it. It's huge and violent in an abstract, almost science-fiction way. There are charred bodies and rubble, machines, fields being overrun, all in smoky gray and metallic colors that bleed into orange and green in the corners. It's amazing.

"Wow," Callie says. "This is huge."

I read the description: *Burn, Baby, Burn* by Matta, an artist from Chile. More props to my people.

"It's about the Watts riots." I read from the placard. In 1965, a highway patrol officer pulled over a black man on charges of drunk driving, which prompted huge protests. Thousands of people took to the streets and began rooting and raging against the racial discriminatory practices of the police department.

"Crazy," she says, reading over my shoulder. "You'd think things would have changed by now."

I look around and don't see any signs, so I take a photo.

"You really like it, huh?" she asks.

"Well, yes, but the photo is for Luis."

"Ah, your new best friend."

"Ha. Yeah," I say.

"I can't believe you have to work with him. You guys are so different."

I don't disagree, but I'm curious as to what Callie means.

"How so?" I ask.

"He's kind of cocky and a jerk and . . . you're neither of those things." She walks away from me and waits at the edge of the room.

I stay where I am in front of the mural, doing my best to act as if I'm still interested in the artwork, as if what she said doesn't matter. Eventually I pull myself away.

"Come on," I say. "Let's go look at the Japanese art. There's something cool over there I think you'll like."

Netsuke are miniature sculptures that the Japanese wore to fasten containers on the sides of their kimonos that would act as pockets. Inside a small room are rows and rows of netsuke. Sunlight streams in from the huge surrounding windows, bathing them in its light. Callie walks slowly through the rows.

"These are my favorite," she says softly. It's the type of room that commands reverence and makes you want to whisper like you're in church.

This is the third time Callie has called something her favorite today, and I smile. I'm beginning to understand she uses that word loosely.

"I thought the *Breathing Light* exhibit was your favorite."

"It was until I saw these." She bends down to get a closer look at one. She catches her breath. "Look at these. Turtles! I love turtles."

I stand alongside her and see three small turtles stacked on top of one another.

"I used to have one of those baby turtles," she says. "You know, the little ones that are illegal to sell on the street? We didn't know that at the time. My mom and I were on Olvera Street for something and there was a woman selling these tiny, adorable turtles, so I begged Mom and she bought one for me. It only lasted a couple of months because I'm pretty sure it was sick. But it was so cute."

"I like this guy." I show her the little octopus, but she's already moved on to something else.

"A snail. A tiny snail. Oh my gosh. These are amazing," she says.

"Here's an entire city carved into an oyster shell."

"How did they do this?"

"No idea," I say.

"It's amazing." She squeals again. "A baby elephant."

Callie is the happiest I've ever seen her, so I'm pretty sure that's a good thing. She touches my arm. "I want one."

And if I could, I would have stolen one right there for her.

After we check out all of the Picassos, I take Callie to the museum's coffee bar. I order us two hot chocolates, since she doesn't drink coffee, and since it's a little cool outside. We walk over to the grass near the La Brea Tar Pits and sit down.

"I never come here," she says when we sit down. "Why do I never come here?"

I pull out the food I packed for us: yogurts, apples, and turkey sandwiches. "Hope this is okay. There's no peanuts."

"Are you kidding? It's great."

We eat in a comfortable silence for a few moments. It's nice to be able to just sit quietly with someone.

"Hey, how'd you know I'm allergic to peanuts?" she asks.

"Two truths and a lie."

She nods. "Good memory. We should keep the questions going for our papers. I haven't even started writing mine yet. Have you?"

"No." I have to admit, I forgot about the paper. At some point over the past few days I'd stopped thinking of hanging out with Callie as a school assignment. Now I kind of just want to hang out with her.

"What's your favorite sandwich?" she asks.

"Peanut butter and jelly," I say.

"Aw. Sorry."

"No worries. Turkey's good. What about yours?"

"Nutella and banana. But I like turkey. Thank you for the food, by the way. I should have brought something too."

"No, my treat. I just like being prepared."

"How often do you come here?"

"Once every couple months or so," I say. "Or I go to the MOCA. There's also the Getty. Actually, there are all kinds of art museums in LA. Do you ever go to museums?"

"No. I should, though. It's just so easy to get comfortable doing the same thing every day." She pauses. "Thank you for showing me something different."

"You're welcome," I say, surprised by her graciousness.

If someone would have told me a week ago that Callie and I would be talking art and having a picnic, I'd have said they were crazy. But it feels right, sitting here with her.

She holds up her sandwich and clinks it against mine like we're cheers-ing after a toast and takes a bite.

"This is good," she says with her mouth full.

And it is.

She points to my bag. "Is your sketchbook in there?"

"Yeah."

"Can I see it?"

I hand it to her, both excited and nervous that she's interested in my art. I watch as she flips through different drawings. She stops on a pair of hands.

"Whose are these?"

"My mom's." I must have ten sketches of her hands in there.

"You like drawing them."

"It's more like I'm practicing, trying to learn and get better each time I draw them. It's something I learned studying Van Gogh."

"Isn't that the guy who cut off his ear?"

I nod. "That's usually the only thing people know about Van Gogh, which is sad. I mean, he did get a little unhinged later in life, but he wasn't a madman. And his process was so amazing. He was completely self-taught and he believed his paintings were studies—that's what he called them. Almost as if he were rehearsing and practicing for the later paintings of his career. And with his portraits, he tried something that was really different for his time. He didn't want to just paint what he saw. He wanted to capture the essence of a person, the internal part that informs the external. So he had to love what it was that he was painting, whether it was a blade of grass or a woman. It's like you need to feel something before you can paint it, and then you paint what you feel. I totally get it." I look up to see Callie watching me closely, and I feel my face grow hot. "Sorry."

"What are you sorry for?"

I shrug. "I don't usually get to talk about art this much." Then, to keep her eyes off me and back on my sketches, I show her the first picture I drew of my mom's hands. "See, the proportions are all off here. I was just getting the outline. If you look, you'll see the progression." I flip ahead to the ones I drew most recently. "Do you see the difference?"

"Yeah. Somehow you've made them look strong, as if they could hold anything, but also fragile, as if they could break with the slightest pressure." She looks at me. "You love your mom."

I smile. Callie's right, but thinking about my mom makes me sad because of what I know.

I change the subject.

"Van Gogh actually believed that all art is motivated by love," I say.

"And what do you believe?" Callie asks me.

I've never been asked this before. At least, not in an artistic context. I'm not sure what to say.

"Sorry, maybe that was too personal." She gives me an out and I take it. For now.

Then she asks me another question. "What was the last thing you drew?"

Before I can stop her, she turns to one of the later pages, which has a picture of Luis turning into a zombie and losing his limbs. I particularly enjoyed digging out the craters on his face and peeling off slabs of flesh. I drew this in Mr. Fisher's class with Greyson's wholehearted approval. He especially loved the dangling flesh pieces. He actually helped me make them look more authentic.

"Whoa, Neruda." She makes a face.

I'm not usually this dark with my art, but Luis brings out the worst in me. "It's bad, I know."

"No, it's really good, but kind of gross," she says. "I like it." She flips again and finds her eyes, but she doesn't recognize them. "Who's this?"

"Oh, I'm just practicing eyes. They're the hardest to get."

"I bet. So, any idea what you're going to draw next?"

"I could draw you, if you like?" I take back my sketchbook and start the outline of her hair on a clean page.

"Here? Now?" She looks around as if someone is watching us.

"Yeah. It's perfect."

"How should I pose?" She leans back and tries to look seductive and laughs. "No, seriously, you're drawing me now?" Her voice catches and I can tell she's nervous, which makes me smile. Callie is never nervous.

"Just be natural."

"How's this?" She sits up straight and stares directly ahead at the fake mastodon coming out of the water over by the tar pits.

"Okay. But maybe try not to be so stiff." I reach over and

put her hair behind her ear so I can get a better view of her profile. "Take a deep breath and let it out."

She does, and her body relaxes a little.

"One more time." She rolls her eyes, but she does it.

"I want you to draw me, Jack, like one of your French girls," she says in a low voice. She turns toward me with a grin, but I have no idea what she's talking about.

"Seriously? You haven't seen *Titanic*?"

I shake my head and continue to add texture to her hair.

"Who are you? *Titanic* is a classic. Don't you watch any movies?"

"Sure. Just not the ones you do, I guess."

"What's the last movie you watched?"

"*The Wizard of Oz*. With you."

"Besides that."

I'm honestly not a huge movie watcher, so it takes me a few minutes to remember. "I think it was *Moonrise Kingdom*."

"Never heard of it."

"It's by Wes Anderson."

"What's he done?"

"A bunch of stuff. *The Grand Budapest Hotel*, *Rushmore*, *The Royal Tenenbaums*."

"Never seen them."

"Really? They're amazing. Very different, though. They're more stylized."

"What do you like about them?"

"Each frame is kind of like a small portrait. Like you're looking through a diorama, or watching a piece of art come to life or something. And they're funny and quirky, but there's an underlying sadness to them."

"You like sad movies?"

I shrug. "Sometimes. Don't you?"

"I never really thought about it."

"You'd probably like *Moonrise Kingdom* the best, then."

"Why?"

"It's about these two kids who fall in love and try to run away together."

"Hmm. Maybe."

Callie is stiff, sitting too straight. She's not quite relaxed. I try to lighten the mood. "So, how does Jack draw the French girls?"

"Never mind." Callie ducks her head away from me, but not before I see the color rise in her cheeks. Something I said made Callie blush.

"I've never had anyone draw me before," she says.

"Pretend I'm not even here. You're just sitting and thinking about whatever you want to think about."

"Just don't pull a Picasso on me. I don't care what you say, those were some ugly women he painted."

She takes a sip of her hot chocolate. But the longer we sit

there, the less comfortable Callie becomes. She starts fidgeting with her cup, the grass, the edges of her shirt. She begins biting her nails. For someone seemingly so confident, her nervousness feels out of character.

For the first time today, I think of Autumn and how completely different she and Callie are. I try to remember what it was that I saw in Autumn in the first place. A pretty face? I'm honestly not sure. Callie is pretty, but she's more than that too. She's talented and competitive and beautiful and she's here with me. She's real. Callie is real. This thought both excites and terrifies me.

Callie is still fidgeting.

I decide to try something. Give her something that might help her feel more comfortable, less aware that she's being studied, drawn. It didn't work on Autumn, but Callie is different.

I reach into my bag and pull out *Twenty Love Poems and a Song of Despair*. I hand it to Callie.

"What's this?" she asks. "He has your name."

"Yeah, remember that poet I'm named after?"

"You carry this around with you?" she says like it's a strange thing.

"Yeah."

"You've read this a lot," she says of the paper so soft, the cover is almost coming off, and the pages dog-eared so frequently, they practically fold themselves. "I'm not really into poetry."

"Have you ever read Neruda?"

"Nope."

"Just give it a try. How about you read and I'll draw."

Callie eyes me skeptically, then crosses her legs and opens to the middle of the book. I hear her voice in my mind, speaking The Poet's words, because I've memorized most of them. The lines thread through the noise of the city like they're weaving a tapestry: the cars passing, people walking by, my pencil drawing the contour of Callie's jaw.

After about twenty minutes, Callie puts down the book and wants to see what I've drawn. I don't want to show her yet because it's not finished, but I relent.

"Wow."

She touches the page with her finger, tracing the outline of her face.

"It'll get better," I say as if to explain away the raw imperfections. "I didn't get to spend as long as I'd like, but it was enough to get a base going."

"No, it's good," she says. "What did you write in the corner?"

"*Callie, Study Number One.*"

"I like that, being studied. You know, you're very intense when you draw. Very focused."

I nod.

"Can I have this?"

"No, I still need to finish it." It's a decent first attempt, but her eyes still evade me. It'll take me forever to understand and draw those eyes. But because she looks disappointed, I say, "I'll give it to you when I'm done, though."

"Deal," she says with a slight smile. She hands me back *Twenty Love Poems*.

"No, you keep it."

She puts it in her bag. "You know, you're full of surprises, Neruda."

"Nah." I return her smile. "I'm an open book."

WE TOGETHER

Callie and I leave the museum and I take her to Milk, a great ice cream place close by. The line behind us is out the door.

"Is the line always this long?" Callie asks.

"Yes. Well, every time I've been. I've been here a bunch with my dad . . ." My voice trails off. I don't want to think about my dad because that'll make me think about how I feel like punching him in the gut. I wonder if he ever took Leslie here. Or were they more discreet? Meeting only in seedy hotels like some cheap cliché. I get a sick feeling. What if they met at my house? I think about how many days I came home after school last year to find Dad already there. Had Leslie been there too?

Did she just sneak out a window? Or did she wait until I wasn't looking to sneak out the front door?

"Hey," Callie says, waving her hand in front of my face. "Earth to Neruda. You okay?"

I look at her. "Yeah. Sorry."

"You do that a lot. Go somewhere else."

"I'm just thinking."

She eyes me like she's concerned. "About what?"

"Just . . . there's just some stuff going on with my family." I don't really feel like talking about it with her. Everything's going so well. I don't want to ruin it.

"Got it. Well, if you need to talk about it . . ."

She offers but she doesn't push, which I appreciate. I'll add that to the growing list of things I'm learning about Callie Leibowitz.

"So, what should I get?" she asks.

"I really like the salted caramel macaroon sandwich."

"Ooh, anything with salted caramel is heaven." Callie's eyes scan the large chalkboard menu at the front of the store. The 1950s red, black, and white decor makes it seem as if you're back in time.

"They have everything!" Callie says.

When we finally get to the front, I decide to try something new and order the Thai tea macaroon ice cream sandwich. She goes for red velvet. As if we've timed it perfectly, a family of three gets up from one of the few tables outside just as we exit, and we dart for the available seats.

"Awesome. Now we can people watch," Callie says. "People are so interesting. You've got your dudes"—she nods to three skinny guys, two Latino and one white, across the street—"couples, families. Did you see that cute old couple holding hands in line? I love how no one in LA looks the same. Can you imagine living in a small town where everyone was just like you? No, thanks."

"Sometimes when I'm out with my sketchbook, I purposely pick people who are totally different from me. I try to draw their story."

"I know what you mean. When I create my faces, I like to think about what story I'm trying to tell through the image. I didn't know people did that with paintings. Hey, the Grove's not far from here, right?" she asks.

"Not too far down the road." I point in the direction.

"We go there on the weekends sometimes. Mom likes the Farmers Market."

She pauses for a minute. I never knew how chatty Callie is.

"This is probably the best thing I've ever tasted." She takes another bite, which draws my attention to her mouth. Her lips are now covered in red velvet.

"The best," I say, but I drop my eyes when she looks at me.

"I'd gain like twenty pounds if I lived near here. How's yours?"

"Want a bite?" I offer.

"Sure."

She leans in and takes a small bite of the macaroon. Suddenly it feels so much like we're on a date that I start to think we're on a date and get nervous. Does she think we're on a date? *Are* we? How can I tell? Should I have paid for her ice cream? I didn't; does that mean she's upset? She doesn't seem upset. Would I want to date Callie?

"Mmm, yours is good too," she says. "How long do you think it would take us to come and sample every dessert they have? A month?"

"Depends. Are we talking about just one a day? Or more? You'd probably get sick of them pretty quickly."

"Impossible, this is amazing. Seriously, heaven just exploded in my mouth right now."

"You're very expressive."

Callie laughs. "My parents say I have a flair for the dramatic."

"I can see that."

"Oh, really."

"Yeah, the way you stomp into class."

"I don't stomp."

"Are you kidding? You definitely stomp."

She gives me a look that I can't quite read. "Maybe I stomp a little."

I laugh. If this is a first date, I'd say it's going very well.

"I have a question for you," she says. "Remember when you said that your best friend is an ex-con? What's that about?"

Callie listens intently, but after I finish telling her about the history of Ezra and me, she looks confused.

"So he's, like, normal?"

"What do you mean?"

"I've never known anyone in prison." She takes another bite and quickly wipes the ice cream from the corners of her mouth with a napkin. "I only know it from TV shows and movies. And most convicts seem kind of messed up."

"He looks like a normal guy, if that's what you mean. He's just trying to figure everything out now, like where he fits and what he should be doing," I say.

"After being locked up for ten years like that, how do you even begin to try to reenter society? Finding a job would be so hard. And can you imagine dating after all that? Unless he had a girlfriend while he was in there. Do you know there are women who actually seek out and date inmates? It's a thing. There are even dating sites devoted to it. You can click on a guy's picture and go to his profile. They even get married to prisoners. It's crazy."

"And you know this how . . . ?"

"My mom. She worked with inmates a few years ago."

"Weird. I'm pretty sure Ezra didn't date anyone in prison. The last person was this girl named Daisy from high school.

He thought they would be together forever, like they were soul mates or something, but he went to prison and she went to college in Santa Barbara."

"That's sad. But it's not like they would have stayed together, especially being that young. And anyway, soul mates aren't real."

It feels as though Callie has just punched me in the gut. She chomps on a piece of cookie, but she might as well be tearing into my soul.

"What do you mean, they're not real?"

"Think about it. That would imply that out of the billions of people on the planet, you're destined to be with just one person. That's insane."

"I don't think so."

"Come on, Neruda. You're telling me you believe that there is one perfect person out there for you and only you?"

"Well . . . kind of . . . yeah."

"No way. It's more like you have people in your life for a certain time and then you move on. I mean, people fall in and out of love all the time, they marry, they divorce, they marry someone else. Does that mean they made a mistake with the first and the second is their soul mate? Or what about those people who get divorced a second time or a third and remain single? Does that mean their soul mate is still out there and they'll know as soon as they meet each other? Highly doubtful."

I'm completely floored by this. "So . . . you don't believe in love?"

"Of course I do. I just don't know about the whole you're-destined-for-only-one-person kind of love. If that were true . . ." She hesitates and stares off.

If that were true . . . I think of Mom and Dad. They were supposed to be soul mates. Now I'm not so sure.

"It has more to do with choice, I think," she says. "Who you choose to love. You make a choice. When people break up, that's a choice too."

Right now, I choose not to have a breakdown.

"Sorry. I don't mean to lay all my baggage on you. You obviously believe in all this stuff." She removes The Poet's book from her bag and pushes it across the table to me. "Are you seeing someone? Or interested in anyone?"

I choke down my ice cream. "No."

"You're not into Autumn Cho?"

"What? No, why would you think that?" I rack my brain trying to remember if I mentioned Autumn to Callie at some point.

"Your sketchbook had some pictures of her."

Crap. "Oh, well, I draw all kinds of things. Meaningless things. A tree. A plastic bag. Autumn's got good bone structure."

She nods, but I'm not sure if she buys it.

"What about you?" I ask. "Are you interested in anyone?"

"No. Not really."

Our pronouncements of nos mark the end of our conversation. But I want to take mine back, because all of a sudden I feel like we've decided something I didn't know we were deciding. My book looks small and damaged on the table between us.

"I told myself at the beginning of the school year I was going to focus on school and volleyball. I don't have time for guys. It's better, don't you think?"

"What?"

"Not having to deal with all of the drama that relationships bring. I mean, seriously, people get so worked up over something that lasts like two weeks."

I can't help but think about Greyson and Mercy. They seemed so perfect, but they broke up too.

"Everyone is crying. Heartbroken," Callie continues. "Friends get involved and have to pick sides. It's not worth it."

"It can be, if it's the right person," I say.

She shrugs. "I'm just saying. It's never worked out for any of my friends."

But something about what she said makes me question if she really meant it.

I change the subject. "So, did you like what you read?"

"I didn't understand all of it. A little steamy. But it's better than what we read in English. It's so hard to figure out the meaning most of the time. I'm horrible at poetry when we have to analyze it in class. I never know what to write."

"I don't think poetry is supposed to be defined and dissected like it's some dead thing. It doesn't work if you try to pin it down and butcher it."

"What do you mean?"

"Well, I'm not sure if we're supposed to understand everything in a poem. I think the point is it's supposed to hit you on a deeper level, a deeper truth that your soul feels even if your brain can't understand it."

Callie stares at me intently. Blink blink stare.

Great. She doesn't believe in soul mates and she doesn't believe in poetry either.

I feel my face grow hot and drop my gaze. "Or, whatever. It's just words."

"Mm-hmm. Words. I've never felt that way about words ever."

"Just . . . here." I push my book back across the table to her. "You may change your mind about love and stuff if you read it," I say lamely. "Please?"

"Doubtful," she says. "But I'll consider it more Neruda research." She picks up the book.

We leave the ice cream shop and she asks me if I have plans the rest of the day.

"No. Why?"

"Movie at my house? We need to continue your film education."

I laugh. "If you say so."

"Hey, *Oz* was awesome, right?"

"It had its moments."

"Well, trust me, you're the romantic, you're gonna love *Titanic*."

All I know about the *Titanic* is that it sinks and almost everyone dies. But if Callie is right, and love is really about taking risks and making choices, I know mine.

"Sounds fun," I say.

WITH ECHOES AND
NOSTALGIC VOICES

"Neruda?"

Callie says my name and I look up. She's bent over The Poet's book, and I'm drawing her. My pencil trembles, moving across the page, as if it's touching flesh rather than paper. The music swells, just like a movie, as Callie glances at me.

"Neruda?" she says again. Her lips move and I'm focused on her lips.

My body is shaking. No. Something's shaking me.

I open my eyes to my parents hovering over me.

"Hey, sleepyhead," Mom says.

"I don't think he's awake yet," Dad says.

I roll away from them.

"You can't sleep the day away," Dad says. He puts his hand on my back and I swat at it, not meaning to hit him, but I do, hard.

"Neruda," Mom starts to say.

"Get up." Dad's tone changes, his voice rough like gravel. "The garage is calling."

"You said it could wait until next weekend." I face him, ready to argue.

"Yeah, well, I changed my mind. And this time go through the bins and boxes against the wall."

"But that'll take—"

"Just do it," he says, and leaves, muttering in Spanish under his breath.

Mom sits on the edge of the bed. "How was last night?"

I stretch and push myself up against the headboard. Last night was interesting, especially when we got to the scene where Jack sketches Rose in the nude. Callie had been joking about me drawing her naked. After that, I kept thinking what it would be like to do it, whether I could handle it. Which means I spent the rest of the night thinking about Callie naked, which is not something you share with your mom.

"It was all right," I tell her.

"Good." She pauses. "Neruda, is something going on between you and Dad that I should know about?"

I freeze but try to act casual, confused. "No. Why?"

She studies me. "You seem upset with him."

I think about telling her, about how good it'll feel to get it off my chest. But I can't. "I'm just tired."

"Are you sure that's all?"

I put on my best everything's-fine face. "Yes, Mom."

She looks at me quizzically, and I can tell she's not buying it.

"I've got to change. Some privacy?" I say, hoping she'll just leave so we can put an end to this conversation before it starts.

"You can talk to me if there's something going on. That boy at school isn't bullying you, is he?"

If only it were that simple.

"No, Mom, everything is fine."

Our garage can hold two cars, but neither of my parents has ever parked there. The only vehicles inside are my scooter and the three mountain bikes that hang from hooks in the ceiling. I haven't ridden my bike in almost a year, since I first got my scooter, even with all of the new bike lanes around our city.

Instead, we fill the garage with clutter, and Dad cleans it out once a year. I just sweep and make it look neat. Clearly, having to go through the bins is my punishment.

I click the opener and the door rises to reveal a large stack of bins against the wall. Each one is labeled in thick black ink with the words PAINT SUPPLIES, CAMPING GEAR, PHOTO BOOKS, or MISC.

This has to be some kind of parental authority abuse. Why do I have to be the one to go through the stuff? Technically it's not even mine. I shake out a black trash bag. What I should do is throw everything away. That'd make my life easier, though Dad just might go crazy if I do. He's into grounding and consequences. In my opinion, he's the one deserving of punishment.

I grab a broom and try to recall details from the dream I was having earlier.

Callie Leibowitz.

I say her name slowly, feel the syllables as they roll off my tongue. *Cal-lie Leee-bo-witz.* There is something about her name. The way your whole mouth is involved in saying it. It's a strong name. Strong like Callie. I wonder if she has a middle name.

After sweeping the garage, I put my earbuds in and listen to some music. Then I set up a small blue beach chair and get to work on the box with the camping gear. There are lamps, a portable stove, matches, utensils, and pots and pans. Everything still looks good. We haven't actually gone camping in years, so I don't spend a lot of time on the stuff. I close the bin and push it back against the wall.

I open the bin labeled MISC. How am I supposed to know what to keep and what to toss? Inside are a bunch of papers, notebooks, and envelopes. It's all my mom's stuff from when she was in college. Binders with her notes from classes. Why does she still have all of this? When I'm done with a class, everything goes in the trash.

As I'm sorting papers, I come across a manila envelope with Dad's name on it. I open it and find letters he's written to Mom.

In the first letter I read, he goes on and on about how amazing Mom is and how lucky he is to have found her. I read another. And another. There are echoes of The Poet in his words, like the line about him being a house with windows that ache for her. It's kind of cool that Mom has kept the letters all these years, but it only makes me feel worse for her.

I read another letter where Dad apologizes for being late. Another where he says he never knew real love before he met her, and how he is certain that they have a love that will last forever.

There are movie ticket stubs. U2 and Prince concert stubs. Pressed flowers.

It looks like Mom kept everything from when they were dating. When did it stop, I wonder. The notes? The proclamations of love? The poetry? When's the last time Dad wrote her a love letter?

I hold a note up to my nose. The ink has long since dried and the smell is now of stale air.

Love is supposed to be a fire, an all-consuming passion that keeps you up at night. A state of being that drives you crazy because you wake to thoughts of her, and end the day with the same. Love is marked by sighs and stars. With songs and butterflies that make your stomach flip and flutter when she looks at you. You feel nervous and excited at the same time. You just want to be near her. You don't even care if you're doing anything—just sitting next to her is good enough.

And the evidence of love is that you become a better person; she makes you better. It's not supposed to be measured by lies and betrayals, smoke and mirrors.

I can't help but wonder: If Callie is right, and love is a choice, when did my dad change his mind?

For a moment, I imagine setting the letters on fire and dropping them into the box until it all goes up in flames. Better to burn out than fade into dust and darkness.

Inside the house, Dad is bent over the tub, cleaning the upstairs bathroom.

I press the corner of the envelope into my thigh. Then, with a flick of my wrist, I toss the envelope at him.

"You might want to read these," I say.

He starts to respond, but I press play and I'm lost in "Us Against the World" by Coldplay.

I can hear him call my name, but it's like I'm underwater. I swim deeper inside a song that explains exactly how love should be. Two people facing the world together. The only thing that matters is their love. A love that is alive, not crumpled and dusty, withered by time and betrayal.

I hear him call out again and again, but I head to my room and dive deeper into the music until I'm so far from shore, he's not even a distant speck on the horizon.

WHAT WE ACCEPT
WITHOUT WANTING TO

After school on Tuesday, Luis and I are supposed to meet in the library to check out our potential space. As usual, he's late.

I stand facing the wall—the canvas, so to speak. Sometimes a blank canvas can be intimidating because it represents all possibilities, and once you start, those options begin to narrow with each choice. But I like the challenge. The idea that in a few hours or weeks there'll be something permanent, something on display that I will have brought into existence is thrilling. It gives me more pleasure and more confidence than anything I'm learning in school. When I'm creating art, I'm doing what I was born to do. There's nothing more satisfying than that and I feel a buzz of excitement. It's almost enough to make me forget about everything going on at home. About having to work with Luis.

"You haven't started anything yet?" Luis walks up.

I look at him like he's kidding, but he's staring like his presence is God's gift to me or something.

"What?" he asks.

"Never mind." The less I have to talk to him, the better.

We tape up the corners and the baseboards with blue tape and cover the floor in front with a tarp. I'm grateful that both of us wear earbuds.

We start on opposite sides, painting the wall with an off-white primer before we attempt the mural design. When we're finished, we observe the clean white wall.

"Looks like it could use another coat."

"Yeah, so how long do you think this is going to take? Until we're done with the whole thing, I mean," Luis asks.

"Well, the unveiling is in four weeks."

"Dude, I can't be spending every day after school like this. I have conditioning."

"So why don't you quit," I mumble under my breath.

"What's that?"

"Nothing. We might be able to punch it out in two if Fisher lets me miss his class a few days."

"I don't think I can miss last period. I've got a borderline C, and I need to get that up for wrestling," Luis says. "What this wall really needs is some spray paint."

"Maybe we could add some in the end. You know, around the edges, to give it more of that street art look, if it sticks with the integrity of the work."

Luis nods and looks at the wall. "Integrity? You mean, like, its truth?"

"Sort of. Every piece of art has an intentionality."

He looks at me, confused.

"Like, what the art is trying to tell the viewer, or the artist's point of view. Something that will be clear even when we're not here to explain it. As long as you don't violate that, anything is game."

Luis's quizzical look remains unchanged.

"We could try to make some spray paint fit with the style of the piece," I say in more simplistic terms for him.

"Whatever. I just think it'll look cool, because if my name's going on it, it better look good. I don't want to come back after graduation and see some lame mural. It needs to be epic."

If Luis thinks I'm going to let him turn this mural into a canvas for his tagging, he's delusional. This is supposed to be *my* legacy.

We're just starting to clean the brushes in the sink of the bathroom when he says, "Shit, it's already four?" He looks at his phone. "I'm going to be late."

He leaves without helping me clean up the rest. Figures.

When I finally get to the parking lot, my scooter won't start. I try and try but nothing works. I text Ezra to see if he can come over tonight and help me fix it.

I think about texting Mom for a ride home, but she doesn't get off work until six. Instead of texting Dad, I walk the scooter all the way to the Metro station.

HOW MUCH HAPPENS
IN A DAY

It's after dark by the time Ezra comes over. "What's the problem?" he asks.

"I don't know. I can't get it to start."

"Did you check the belt?" He bends down next to my scooter in the garage and tinkers with it.

"Yeah," I say like I know what he's talking about.

Dad comes out through the kitchen door and throws away the trash. "Hi, Ezra." He avoids my eyes. We have fallen into a pretty solid routine of avoiding each other. I'm not proud of how I've been acting, but I don't know what else to do. I expected my dad to face the situation, not run from it like a coward. It makes me wonder if I know him at all and what else he might be hiding from us. He is not the man I thought he was.

"Hi, Carlos." Ezra stands to greet him.

"How are you?"

They shake hands. Dad looks so old standing there next to Ezra. Old and tired and run-down. What did Leslie see in him?

"Good, thanks. Neruda asked me to check out his bike for him."

"Oh, is there something wrong with it?" Dad asks with a tone that implies he could have done something to help. Dad wouldn't even know how to check a car's engine or change a flat tire. I can do both of those things thanks to Ezra.

"The belt just needs some more tension," Ezra says after inspecting it for like three seconds.

"How'd you get so good with auto mechanics?" Dad asks.

Ezra shrugs. "Runs in the family, I guess."

Before Dad can ask another question, I cut him off. "Dad, we have stuff to do." I turn and pretend I'm doing something to the scooter.

"Right. Okay. Good to see you, Ezra." He gives Ezra a hug and a pat on the back. "Chao."

Dad goes back inside the house while Ezra finishes with my scooter.

"Want me to soup it up for you? Put on some hydraulics? Impress the ladies?"

"Shut up," I tell him. Though I wonder what Callie would think about it. If it would impress her.

"Like new," he says a little while later. He wipes his hands on a rag. "Do you think your dad will ever let you have a real bike?"

"You mean a motorcycle? Yeah right. Mom would argue how dangerous bikes can be."

"Does she know this is just as dangerous?"

"She thinks I'm safer because of the speed."

We sit on the two chairs on the porch. It's pretty dim because the light is out and Dad keeps forgetting to replace the bulb.

"So I'm guessing from that little exchange I just witnessed you haven't talked to your dad yet," he says.

"Not really. He asked me not to say anything."

"That's tough."

"Yeah, I don't know what to do. I feel like my mom deserves to know, but if I tell her what I overheard, then what? I mean, she'd probably leave him, right? Why would someone stay with a person who cheated on them?"

"People stay together for all kinds of reasons."

I let this sink in for a moment.

"What do you think I should do?" I ask Ezra.

He hunches over with his hands folded in front of him. "Look, I've made a lot of mistakes in my life, but if there's one thing I learned from Rafa and everything, it's knowing when to speak and when to remain silent."

"So you don't think I should tell my mom?"

"I'm not saying you should or shouldn't. I just think you need to be careful and really think about what's at stake here."

We sit in the front yard and watch the occasional car pass by. For a long time I think through Ezra's advice. It's not about right or wrong here. It's about something else, like figuring out the best thing for everyone. The problem is, I have no idea what that is.

After Ezra leaves, I bypass my parents on the couch in front of the TV. Mom offers to make popcorn, but I fake like I have homework to do. They've never seen me so studious before.

"You sure everything's all right?" she asks.

"Yeah, just got a lot to do."

"You're not feeling sick, are you?"

"No, Mom. I'm fine, really."

"Okay. But I'm going to check in on you later," she says.

My dad doesn't say a word.

Once I'm upstairs in my room, I close the door and lean against it. Even though it's small, I feel safe; I don't have to hide anything here. I find the pages with Callie's eyes and practice drawing them all night.

For the first time I think I understand The Poet's words

about his lover having oceanic eyes. It's not about the color. Callie's eyes aren't blue, but they are deep and full of something. They pull me in and make me want to know more and see more.

That night I dream of the ocean.

I HAVE GONE MARKING

My phone buzzes. It's Callie.

Can you come over?

When?

Now. Need help with something.

Sure.

In twenty minutes I'm at Callie's front door. Her mom answers on the second knock with Lucy right at her heels. I reach down to pet her.

"Callie's up in her room. Good luck—she's in one of her artistic moods. She tells me you're an artist."

Callie's talking about me to her parents? That's got to be good.

"I am, yes."

"That's nice. The world needs people who aren't afraid to express themselves."

"Neruda. You coming?" Callie yells.

I stumble up the stairs.

Callie's door is cracked just a sliver. She pulls it all the way open just as I'm about to knock.

"Finally! So, what do you think?"

She stands with her hands on her hips, and her face is covered in patches of red, yellow, and blue makeup. Her mouth is pursed like she's either upset or trying to look like a model.

"Umm . . . good?"

"Liar. I thought I'd at least get the truth from *you*."

She slumps down in the chair in front of her makeup mirror. Color and brushes are strewn all over the bed and floor.

Taped up to the mirror is a picture from Picasso's cubist period. It's called *Seated Woman*.

Callie's trying to imitate more than just the woman's makeup, but her facial expression too.

"It's a good attempt," I say. "It just doesn't look like the Picasso piece yet."

"It's not working. The dimensions are all off because, you know, my eyes are the right proportions and so are my nose and mouth."

"Well, what if you try being less literal? And maybe use your whole face."

"Can you try it?" She hands me a tube of black eyeliner.

She turns her face toward me, and I'm suddenly so nervous, I have to shake out my hand first.

"You'll want to look at the planes of my face and draw a line down the middle and then across, like this."

Callie shows me what to do and I make a faint line starting at her forehead. She studies the lines for a second. "Nah. Let's start over." She takes a cloth and wipes her face clean.

"Sorry. I don't have experience doing makeup," I say.

"It's okay. I do and I still can't make this work."

"Well, maybe you're focusing on the wrong thing. I don't think you can have your actual eyes be the eyes of the piece. What if your right eye is over here instead?" I touch the upper part of her right cheek with the makeup brush. "If you paint over or put makeup over your eyelids when you have them closed, that's when it'll look like the painting."

"Yeah, that's what I thought too, but it's hard to do this one on my own. Can you help me?"

"I don't really know how to use all this stuff."

"You can help direct me. Please? I've already been at this for a couple of hours. Here, grab that chair."

She doesn't let me give another excuse.

188

I pull over the chair and sit next to her while she puts on some kind of a base. "Is that your primer?"

She laughs. "Yeah, something like that."

I watch as she begins to apply a coat of makeup across her forehead.

"So, what did I pull you away from?"

"Nothing," I say.

Callie's mom peeks through the door. "How's it going?"

"Fine, Mom."

"Good. Here's some almonds and granola bars in case you guys get hungry." She leaves a tray on Callie's bed. "I'll be out back, okay, sweetie?" She gives Callie a kiss on the top of the head and a hug that goes on a little too long. Callie pats her.

"Okay, Mom. Thanks."

She leaves and Callie says, "Sorry."

"Why?"

"For my mom being weird. It's because I have a boy in my room and she doesn't want any funny business."

I blush thinking about what kind of funny business I could get into with Callie. Is she flirting with me?

Callie starts applying black liner to her face.

"Wait, no, draw the lid here," I point to her cheek again.

"Can you do it?"

I try to draw the eye, but it's hard on skin. I have to hold the bottom of her chin to stabilize her. Or maybe I have to stabilize myself. Callie doesn't even flinch as I hold her face, like she's used to me touching her. I try to move past the fact that I'm touching Callie, that I'm physically closer to her than I've ever been to another girl, and just keep working.

When I'm finished, she looks super creepy, like a lopsided three-eyed creature with one eye under and to the right of her real eye.

"Cool. Can you do the other eye?"

This one I draw a little higher, more on the side of her left eye, but it doesn't look right. "I think you can just use your real eye, but let's make it slant here at the corners and give it the illusion that it's drooping," I say.

Her face is turned up toward me; her eyes are closed. It's almost like she's inviting me to kiss her. At least, that's what we would do if this were a movie or TV. I wonder what kind of kiss it would be. Would it be the slow, drawn-out kind, where two people stare at each other for a long time and slowly lean in and kiss each other while the music swells all around them? Or the I-can't-do-anything-else-until-I've-kissed-you-first kind, where the couple runs into each other from afar? The kind where the guy pushes her up against a wall or a tree because the need and passion are too great to be gentle?

I haven't experienced this kind of kiss before, or any kind actually, but I can imagine what it might feel like. That perfect, right moment. The magic and poetry of it.

Callie's breath falls on my hands as I work. My heart races and my own breath is hot on her face. This could be my moment. I start to lean closer, but she opens her eyes, and I flinch. If she's weirded out by how close I am to her, she doesn't show it.

"Sorry, got an itch." She crinkles up her nose and scratches just to the side of it. She looks at herself in the mirror and giggles. "Awesome. Keep going." She tilts her face up toward me again and closes her eyes.

"So, do you and your mom get along?" I ask. Anything to keep my mind off of her lips, her eyes. How perfect this moment could be.

"For the most part. Sometimes I get so irritated with her when she tries to analyze me. But she has gotten better with that."

"She tries to analyze you?"

"Yeah, like I'm one of her clients. She wants me to talk everything through with her. And she doesn't get that she's my mom. I'm not going to tell her everything." She sighs. "You can't choose the family you're born into, right? What about your mom? You guys close?"

"We're not *not* close. We're normal, I guess."

"What about your dad?"

"He's okay."

"You guys don't get along?"

"No, well . . ." I'm not sure if I'm ready for Callie to know about my parents. But she's being open and honest with me, so I decide to be open and honest with her. "I overheard him on the phone the other day talking to another woman. I'm pretty sure he cheated on my mom."

She opens her eyes. "Neruda, that's horrible."

"Yeah, well. It happens, right?"

"Are you okay?"

I shrug. "No, but there's nothing I can do about it, so . . ." Telling her helps let out some of the pressure that's been building inside me. It's different from telling Ezra, more of a risk, and there's such deep concern in her eyes.

She puts her hand on my arm. "Thank you for telling me. I'll pray for you guys. I hope you don't think that's cheesy."

"No. But I thought you weren't religious."

"I'm not. It doesn't mean I don't pray."

"Thanks," I say, touched.

"You're welcome."

I work on Callie's left eye, trying to make it droop. A comfortable silence settles over us as I turn her face into a cubist painting.

A few minutes later, I finish. "There. Why don't you take a look."

She examines her reflection for a moment before exclaiming, "I look like a freak show!"

"Pretty much," I agree.

"You could be a makeup artist if you wanted," she says while she turns this way and that to take it all in.

"No way."

"I'm serious. It's not just a women's field, if that's what you're worried about. Plenty of men are makeup artists," she says. As if that's the reason holding me back.

"Is that what you want to do? Become a makeup artist?" I ask her.

"Depends. I've got my top five schools picked out and a few others as backups. I'm really hoping for a volleyball scholarship, but I know that's a long shot. The reality of me getting in somewhere like USC is pretty slim, but there's all kinds of private and small schools that are looking to improve their athletic teams. Also, if I go out of state, I have a better chance. I'm looking into some makeup academies too, but my parents want me to do the traditional school thing first. How about you?"

"I'm thinking about art school."

"You haven't started researching?"

"I mean, a little. There's the Art Center in Pasadena."

"Great school. It's super competitive, though. You'll need a portfolio. You should definitely put the mural thing in there. Any school would be super impressed."

"It'll happen if it's meant to, I guess."

"What does that mean?"

"I just mean if I'm supposed to get in, I'll get in."

She looks at me as if in shock. "It doesn't just happen that way, Neruda. First, you have to fill out an application, then do an in-person interview, visit the school, get the right grades, get the right test scores, volunteer. And sometimes that's still not enough. It's not like you can just sit around and expect it to happen. You have to *make* it happen."

It's the quickest I've ever heard Callie speak. Her words rush at me like a river. I hold the back of the chair as if not to be swept away.

"Have you even visited a campus?" she asks.

"No."

"Neruda, this is serious. You need to go as soon as possible. You should also schedule a meeting with an admissions person too. And bring your parents. And dress really nice. I can help you pick something out."

"Have you always been this intense?"

"This is not intense. This is reality," she says.

Suddenly I feel completely overwhelmed. What have I been doing? I don't even have a portfolio ready to go.

"Sorry. I didn't mean to scare you. It's just . . . I take this stuff really seriously and I've been under a lot of pressure lately. I didn't mean to lay all that on you."

"It's okay."

"Would you mind taking my picture?" She hands me her

camera and faces the lens square on, serious. I show her the photo so she can approve. She stares at it awhile, then turns away from me.

"Are you all right?"

She shrugs her shoulders and wipes her eyes. "You ever feel like . . . it's all just a lot? I practice every day till five, plus schoolwork. I work really hard, but I'm just not that straight-A student, or B or even C."

She glances at me. Tears streak the sides of her face and blend the colors together.

"Sometimes I wish I could just go to sleep and wake up in some magical place. Like Dorothy in Oz." She laughs. "That probably sounds dumb."

"No. It sounds like . . . a great escape. I'd go with you," I say.

She smiles, then looks at herself in the mirror. "Ahh. Well, at least you took the picture before this." She starts to clean off the smears of her makeup with a wipe.

Even if I was only Toto, I'd go just to be near her.

"Thanks, Neruda. You're a really good friend."

I smile. I suppose I should be happy with that label, considering not long ago we had barely even spoken. Somehow, though, the word is hollow and echoes against the walls of my chest. It's a good word, but here in her bedroom, it's the last thing I want to be.

THE WEARY ONE

After leaving Callie's house, I'm confused. I think about calling Greyson for advice, since he is my friend with the most relationship experience, but decide I need more of a man's opinion on the situation. I call Ezra.

"If a girl invites you to her house to help her with something and you have a great time and she says that you're a good friend, do you think that means she just wants to be friends?" I ask when he answers.

"Maybe."

"I just don't understand girls. I mean, how do you know if they even like you?"

"Have you talked to this girl?"

"Yes, we talk all the time. And then she calls me and I come over and help her and touch her face and everything and she says we're such good friends."

"You touched her face?"

"She asked me to help her with some makeup painting thing."

"Hmm."

"I don't want to be just friends."

"Does she know that?" Ezra asks.

"I mean, I haven't exactly come out and told her."

"Maybe you need to be a little bolder, get some *ganas*, let your actions speak for themselves. Ask her out on a date. What does she like?"

"Movies."

"Take her to the movies, then."

"I think I've waited too long. There's the initial getting-to-know-you stage where you determine what kind of relationship you're going to have, and Callie's clearly put me in the friend zone."

"Nah, you just gotta ask her out. Be direct, man. Girls like that instead of playing some game."

"Is that what you did with that girl from high school? Daisy?"

He pauses for a minute. "I don't remember."

"Come on. How did you even meet her?"

"We were part of the same group of friends. I don't remember the first time I met her; it was more like suddenly I noticed she was there."

"That's how it was with Callie."

"She used to babysit for this family with twins on Friday nights, and she was always whining about how hard it was. This one night I got the address from her sister and showed up with a pizza and flowers."

"What kind of flowers?" I ask.

"White daisies."

"Ha."

"I was very clever," he says.

"So . . . ?" I say, urging him to continue.

"So, she didn't let me inside because boys weren't allowed without an adult present, but she did take the flowers. I think I stood in front of that open doorway for like five minutes before I finally bailed. But it broke the ice. I was persistent, and three weeks later we were going out."

"Did you ask her out or did it just happen?"

"Nothing just happens. I probably said something smooth like, 'You want to go out?'"

"Did she say yes right away or did she have to think about it?"

"She said yes and then I kissed her."

"Where did it happen?"

"At her cousin's house in the backyard."

"How'd you know you were in love with her?"

"I knew it the moment I kissed her."

"But how?"

I want to ask him if it was an epic kiss. Did it stop time and space and knock the breath out of him? I imagine this happening with Callie, that it'll be one of those moments that will forever change my life.

"You just know."

"That's what everyone says." I sigh. But what about when you think you know and it doesn't work out? I thought I knew with Autumn, but I realize I never even knew Autumn, not like I know Callie. Autumn was just a crush, a pretty face. Things with Callie are . . . different.

"You should go for it now, man, while you can," Ezra says.

I can hear the regret in his voice, and it's then I remember our deal. So what if nothing ever happened with Autumn; I'm definitely trying to put myself out there. Big-time.

"You think any more about contacting Daisy?" I ask.

Ezra doesn't respond.

"Do you ever think she might have been your soul mate?"

"Neruda," he sighs. "I haven't seen her in ten years."

"Don't you think you owe it to yourself to at least see if there's still the possibility? At least look her up and check if she's married. What if she's been waiting for you all this time?"

"It doesn't matter."

"Why not?"

"Because I've moved on. I had to."

"What's her name?"

"Who?"

"The girl you've moved on with."

He doesn't give me a name because I know there's no girl.

"If Daisy was the one, she might still be the one, right?"

"It doesn't work that way."

"Why not?"

"Because, man, some forevers don't last."

And it's the saddest thing I've ever heard Ezra say.

HERE I LOVE YOU

During art class, Mr. Fisher lets me out to work on the mural. We've got less than three weeks left before the library dedication, so we have to work quickly. Mr. Fisher has also worked his teacher privilege magic to get Luis out of last period. Now Luis is reclining in an orange chair with his earbuds in, picking a zit, while I outline a section of the mural.

Typical.

I try to focus on my work and forget about my conversation with Ezra last week. Try not to think about what he said and that he might be right—that most relationships don't last. Because last night, I found her—his Daisy. She was easy to locate. She's a teacher in Santa Barbara. I sent Ezra the link to her school's web page. Ball's in his court now.

After forty-five minutes or so, Mr. Fisher comes in to check on us. "Neruda? A word?"

I get off the ladder and follow him around a corner.

"What are you doing?"

"Drawing," I say, wondering if this is some sort of a trick question.

"What is Luis doing?"

I shrug.

"Look, he can't sit there the whole time and just watch you. The goal is that he actually collaborates with you on this project."

"I was just getting down all of our dimensions."

"Please let Luis help you. You need to work together if you're going to finish this in time."

"Fine," I say.

Mr. Fisher leaves and I approach Luis. He removes his earbuds.

"Your turn."

He grins.

"You can take this whole section." I point to the city on the mock-up of the mural taped to the wall. "I'll start here." I point to one of the portraits. "See where I've marked the perimeters? It's loose, so it doesn't have to be exact, but try to stick to the boundaries."

He grunts.

"Don't screw it up," I say. "I don't want this to take any longer than it needs to."

Luis climbs the ladder and flings a little paint at the wall. "Oops."

"What are you doing?"

"Relax," he says. "I'll paint over it later."

I put my earbuds in so I don't have to listen to anything else he says.

We keep working through last period. Greyson stops by before his water polo practice and gives me an approving head nod. He also suggests I may want to think about adding a disemboweled body in the middle of the grass. After another hour, Luis and I make pretty good headway on the mural. This time, I make sure he helps me with the cleanup before he leaves.

It's almost five o'clock and I remember Callie mentioning that volleyball practice lets out at five, so I have just a small window to cross paths with her. I figure the more I interact with her, the more chances I'll have at winning her over. And even though our relationship is platonic at this point, I've been physically closer to her and stared more deeply into her eyes than any other girl.

In my mind, I rewrite the scene where I'm helping her apply

makeup in her bedroom. She starts crying and talking about all the pressure she feels. I say her name. She turns toward me with her eyes all glossy and sad, and I bend down to kiss her. When I pull back and look into her eyes again, they tell me that I'm the one. Then we kiss again and again.

I cross the campus and see Callie walking away from the gym.

Ezra said to be direct and don't play games, but we're friends, so I don't want to come across too strong.

I notice Callie alone and walking quickly. I have to jog a little to make sure that we'll run into each other. I keep my head down as though I'm going somewhere specific and don't see her.

"Neruda?" Callie says.

I look up and she waves. Perfect.

"Oh, hey, Callie." I try to act casual, as if running into her is a total coincidence.

As she walks over to me, I can see she's wearing her volleyball workout clothes—some black leggings that cut off at the knees and a tank top, knee pads pushed down to her ankles. Her legs are muscular, especially her thighs.

"What're you still doing here?" she asks.

"I was working on the mural."

"Cool. How's it going?" she asks.

"Good. Um, what are you doing?"

"Practice. We just got out." Her hair is in a ponytail. Her makeup is a little smudged underneath her eyes. I can smell her sweat, which actually turns me on.

"Oh, I didn't realize you had practice on Wednesdays." I wonder if she can read my lie.

She waves to some other volleyball players in the distance.

"Yeah. Every day after school."

"Are you getting a ride with Imogen?" I ask.

"Not today, she's sick. How did you know I ride with her?"

"You told me, remember? In one of our Q-and-A sessions."

"Oh, right."

I shift from foot to foot.

"I could give you a ride if you need one," I say.

"I was going to walk home."

"Oh, cool. I guess you're not too far, right? Like two miles? You could do that easily. You're in great shape."

"Ha. Thanks," Callie says.

If this were a movie, this is the part where it would get awkward. The part where Callie realizes I'm interested in her and she isn't interested back, so we both pretend that I'm not and then we end up not talking to each other again. So far I've managed to avoid the awkward stage with Callie. Maybe she likes me too and is just waiting for a sign that I'm interested in her?

"You're so funny, Neruda," she says.

Funny is good. It's not like she said, *You're a creepy stalker, Neruda.* That would be bad.

"So, you want a ride?"

"Yeah, that'd be good actually. But can we stop and get something along the way?"

"Sure."

Callie gets on the back like she's done before and holds on to the sides of the seat. As we are about to pull out of the parking lot, I hear, "Neruda!"

Greyson is waving across the way.

"Putting in the work!" he yells.

"What'd he say?" Callie asks from behind me.

"Nothing." I'm going to kill Greyson.

We go to the grocery store, where Callie buys a Gatorade, a bag of pistachios, and some stamps.

She opens the bag and eats a couple pistachios. She holds up the bag for me and I take some too. It's like today is just another day of us as "us," and we've been sharing pistachios forever.

She drinks the Gatorade and offers me some. I take a sip after her, very aware that my lips are touching the place where hers were only a second ago. I don't even wipe off the rim when I drink.

"I get so hungry after practice."

She takes another drink and this time she lets out a huge, short but full burp. I can only stare. She laughs hysterically. "Oh my gosh. I'm so sorry."

Her laugh breaks my stare. Then I start cracking up too, because I don't think I've ever heard a girl burp that loudly.

She's laughing so hard that she doubles over and the pistachios she's holding spill to the ground. I immediately bend to pick them up and so does she.

"That was awesome!" I say.

"That was so embarrassing. Don't you ever tell." She points a finger at me and tries to look serious, but her face is red and she's flustered. She starts laughing again.

And all I'm thinking is how perfect she is and that I want this moment to last forever and that I think I might be in love with her. I want her more than anything I've ever wanted in my entire life.

"You okay?" she asks. "You're all pale."

"I'm good." But I want to tell her that I'm better than good. That I'm head over heels for her.

"Seriously, please don't say anything or I'll never speak to you again once this whole thing is over."

"I promise. Not a word," I say, smiling.

"I haven't even started mine yet, have you?"

"What?"

"The assignment," she says.

"Oh. No."

I'd kind of forgotten about the assignment.

"Me neither. I've got my title, though. Want to hear it?"

I do, but suddenly all I can think is: What if the only reason Callie keeps asking me to do stuff is because we've been partnered on some dumb school project, not because she actually enjoys hanging out with me? It's enough to make me wish we had met outside of school. That we had run into each other somewhere else, like we were supposed to meet, like this is fate.

"It's called 'The Enigma of Neruda Diaz.'"

"Oh," I say.

I don't know if her calling me an enigma is a good thing or a bad thing.

"It means there's more to you than meets the eye. And that's a very good thing. Do you have a title for mine yet?"

She tilts her head to the side and smirks, waiting for my answer. Beauty. The Girl Who Stole My Heart. The Only Girl for Me. The One I Long to Be With. "I'm not good with titles."

"Boo," she says. "Just don't have it be my name. That's boring."

"I don't think you could ever be boring."

We finish picking up the pistachios, and she looks at me questioningly.

"Three-second rule," I say, and eat one myself. She follows with the one in her hand.

"Oh, I forgot to give this to you in class." She takes out The Poet's book and hands it to me. "I finished it."

"And?" I put the book in my back pocket.

"And it's good. I like the one about tonight writing the saddest lines."

"How come?"

"'Cause it's about loss, and I think everyone can relate to that. He's writing about loving and losing a woman, but it could be about anything really. That's the one I felt the most connection to," she says.

"My favorite is the one about being still. But my all-time favorite poem of his is 'If You Forget Me.' It's not in this collection. I'll show it to you sometime."

"Cool."

Callie and I are discussing The Poet. And she thinks there's more to me than meets the eye. This day can't get any better. We walk back to my scooter.

"So, um, sorry about the other day," she says.

"What do you mean?"

"When I got all emotional and stressed. Sorry if it freaked you out."

"No freak-out here. I get it."

"You just seem so steady."

I smile. "My act is working."

She smiles back, then turns serious. "So, how is everything going with your parents?" she asks.

"Oh, fine. Dad's going for the husband of the year award."

"I thought you said he cheated."

"Yeah, but my mom doesn't know that."

"Wait a minute." She puts her hand on my arm. "Your dad hasn't told your mom he cheated?"

My skin warms underneath her touch. "Technically he hasn't even admitted it to me. We basically just avoid each other when we're home, so it's not like we've had the chance to have a heart-to-heart."

And I don't want to either. I don't want to hear his weak apology. I don't want to know the why. No why could mend the crack that's formed between us.

"Wow." She drops her hand, but I still feel the place where it had been. "I cannot imagine keeping a secret like that. It would be so hard for me not to tell my mom. First of all, I can't really lie. To my mom especially. I can't hide anything from her."

"I think my mom knows something is up. She keeps asking me if I'm feeling well or if there's something going on at school."

"Have you thought about telling her?"

"I'm not sure it's really my place . . . Can we just . . . Let's change the subject."

"Okay. Sorry."

There's a long pause and neither of us says anything. I hate my dad even more for ruining this moment with Callie.

Then she says, "So, what are you doing for Halloween?"

"No plans."

I haven't done the whole trick-or-treating thing in years. Mom likes it when I help her pass out candy to all the kids. She usually plays "Thriller" on repeat and dresses up like a witch. I usually give her a hard time about it, but this year I'll probably give in. It's the least I can do.

"Well then, you should come with me."

"Where?" I ask.

"It'll be a surprise. Just make sure you wear a button-down shirt and black pants."

"Okay. But you should know I hate surprises," I say.

"Oh, come on. It'll be painless. Think of it as research for your paper."

"Sure," I say, and smile. "Research."

Callie just asked me out.

THERE'S NO
FORGETTING

Mom is hanging out with a couple of her friends tonight, so I heat up some leftover chicken and potatoes and head for my room. There's no way I'm going through the motions with Dad at dinner. I sit on my bed and eat, imagining what Callie might have planned for us on Halloween.

I get a text from Greyson.

DUDE

?

Callie L??

I send him a happy and stressed emoji followed by just friends.

He responds with another DUDE!! and five thumbs-up signs.

There's a knock on my door.

"Come in."

Dad enters.

"Is that your dinner?" He nods to my almost empty plate.

"Yep," I say.

He sits at my desk.

"Neruda, we need to talk."

I don't say anything, just silently wish he would go away.

"Last year, things were rough. Your mother and I were going through something. And I know it's not an excuse, of course, but I'm trying to give this situation the context it needs."

I stare at him. He's talking about context as if we're in one of his courses. He's hunched over, looking at his hands, playing with his wedding ring. Does he take it off when he teaches so that his students don't know he's married? What did he do with it when he was with Leslie?

"I am not proud of what I did, but it happened. It didn't last long and it's over now. It already feels like another lifetime ago."

He glances up at me but quickly drops his eyes to his hands again.

"I ended it and hadn't spoken with her until she called me completely out of the blue. I'm so sorry you had to hear that conversation. But Neruda, *lo juro*, I swear it. There is nothing going on between us. I haven't even had any contact with her for a year now."

"Why are you telling me this? You should talk to Mom. It's not right, lying to her. She deserves to know."

"It would break her heart if she knew."

And what of my heart? I want to ask. My heart is a weak vessel, unsuited for betrayal.

I close my eyes because I just want him to disappear now.

"Neruda, I'm sorry. I hope you will be able to forgive me."

I begin counting in my head. Somewhere between thirty-five and forty, Dad leaves. I open my eyes and stare at the ceiling, let the heat rise and swell around me as warm tears nip at the corners of my eyes. I wipe them away but they keep coming.

THE TRAITOR

In the morning, instead of going to school, I head over to USC. Forty-three minutes later, I'm standing in one of the huge doorways of the Doheny Library. It's not that I've never been here before. Quite the opposite. It's Dad's favorite library on campus. I've sat in the lounge and drawn the ceiling while waiting for him on occasion. I glance upward at the curvatures and thick wooden beams—the architecture the building is known for. Huge lights shine down over all the tables. I quickly survey the room, hoping Dad won't suddenly appear. He should be teaching class, unless he's also lied about his schedule this term.

The room is clear. No sign of Dad, but I remain in the

doorway. The checkered floor spreads out in front of me like a large game of chess. I am still.

"Excuse me," a woman says from behind me, forcing me to move.

I walk with my head down and sit at one of the long rectangular tables. The three other students already sitting there don't even acknowledge me. They're all wearing headphones and taking notes on tablets, reading books.

Looking around, I see a couple of women behind the reference desk. They're wearing name tags, but I can't make them out from where I am. This is stupid. I never should have come.

I take out The Poet's book that Callie returned to me and open it so it'll look like I'm doing something. But instead of reading, I can't stop myself from looking around the room. Students come and go.

Then I hear it.

"Leslie?"

Someone says her name. Two women hunch over a computer screen. I can't tell which one is Leslie from here. I stand up. I walk to the counter with purpose. I just want to get a good look at her. That's all. I want to see the woman who made my dad throw away years of vows and happiness and trust. The one who's probably off screwing another professor in another department.

At the desk, I read the women's name tags. One is Amy. The other one is Morgan.

Maybe I just imagined someone saying Leslie's name.

I quickly drop my head and start to walk away.

"Can I help you?" a woman asks.

I turn and see a girl standing next to me. She moves her black hair to the side and I read her name tag: Leslie de Prieto. Her whole name spelled out in thick black letters.

"Um."

"Anything I can help you find?"

I break out in a sweat. All the words I want to say to her return to the wound that's marked my soul ever since I heard Dad whisper her name.

"I . . . I'm not sure."

Now that she is real and standing in front of me, I have no idea what to do.

"Try me."

She moves to one of the open computers.

"Well, um," I say, following her. "I've got this paper." I'm trying to think of what a college student would say and do.

"For freshman comp?"

Good. She thinks I'm a freshman. "Yeah."

"Okay. So what's your thesis?"

My thesis? I know what that is. It's an argument for a paper. Suddenly my years of being in academic recovery are paying off. I may actually be recovered.

"If you don't have one yet, we can just start with your topic."

Or not. I'm in way over my head here.

"Neruda?" she asks.

"What?" I panic. How does she know my name?

She points to the book I'm holding—*Twenty Love Poems.* "Are you researching Pablo Neruda?"

"Oh. Yes. Yes I am." I hold up the book as if it's a trophy.

She types something into the computer. "Depending upon your research questions, we have most of his collection, plus multiple translations and biographies."

"Biography," I say. Anything to end this conversation quickly.

"All right, I can show you where they are."

Before I can say *That's okay, I'll find it myself,* she's walking toward the stacks. I follow her, completely stuck now.

"What made you pick Neruda?" she asks.

I cannot believe we're having this conversation. Suddenly I feel like everything is wrong. What was I thinking coming here? I'm an idiot.

I say the only true thing I know in the moment. "He's the greatest love poet."

"Ah," she says, and smiles as if she knows something I don't. It's a side smile, the kind that makes you want to know what's behind it. I wonder how many times she and Dad exchanged knowing smiles. The thought makes me sick.

"He's more of a political poet, in my opinion," she continues.

"It's not as apparent in the book you have, the one that made him famous. But if you look at his canon of work, you'll see what I mean. Though I suppose you could argue that even in his political poems, he's motivated by love. Love for nature. Love for his people. Love for his country."

The way she speaks reminds me of Dad, and I want to run. They probably discussed all kinds of writers and literature.

"Not to mention his love of many women. Amazing how history can just write off what a womanizer he was because he was such a great artist."

Leslie takes me to the stacks and pulls out a book. "Maybe start with this one?"

On the cover there's a black-and-white picture of Neruda as he is usually captured: later in life, wearing a hat and sitting with his legs crossed.

"Thanks," I say. The only word I'm able to utter.

"If you need anything else, just let me know." She reaches into her pocket and pulls out a card. "Also, I'm available for tutoring. My specialty is writing, so if you need any additional help for your paper, I'd be happy to."

On the white card is her name, LESLIE DE PRIETO, in bold block lettering, followed by the words ACADEMIC TUTOR and her email and phone number. She walks away from me.

I need to get out of there immediately. When I get outside, I inhale lungfuls of air, trying to steady myself. I don't stop moving until I'm at the Metro station, and my heart races long after I find a seat.

At home I research Pablo Neruda's personal life, focusing specifically on his relationships. I discover he was married three times. How did I never know this? He also had many affairs. I have no idea what to do with this information.

It angers me that Leslie was right. But what angers me more is that The Poet, this great artist who wrote about true love as this powerful, life-changing force, was a liar. What right does he have to speak about everlasting love? How could he write such lines of pure conviction about one love and then betray himself with another on the next page? How can you love someone with all your being and then love another the same way?

I slam my computer shut and stare at Papi's old collection of Neruda's books on the shelf. The words that have been passed down from father to son.

My phone rings. It's Ezra.

I take a deep breath and answer.

"What're you doing?" he says.

"Nothing."

The wail of a siren comes through the phone, so it's hard to hear him.

"Where are you?" I ask.

"Walking. Hey, you think your parents will let you go camping with me next weekend?"

Yes. Anything to get me away. Away from this house. This mess. All of it.

"Where do you have in mind?" I ask.

"Santa Barbara."

DOWN THROUGH THE
BLURRED SPLENDOR

The whole next week, I do my best to shake off thoughts of Leslie, thoughts of Dad, even thoughts of The Poet. The only thing getting me through the week is the promise of going away. That, and Halloween.

On Halloween night, I show up at Callie's door at 5:00, like she told me. I'm also wearing nice black pants and a long-sleeve white button-down shirt that really needs to be ironed. I try to smooth it out as I'm standing on Callie's doorstep, but she answers before I make much progress. She comes to the door in a long white old-fashioned skirt with a red corset at the waist and a white blouse that exposes both shoulders. Her hair is curled and pinned up in the front, and down in the back. A couple of curls hang over the front of her bare shoulders. There's glitter all around her eyes, and her lips are a ruby red.

"Well?" She poses with one hand against the door frame, the other on her waist.

I take a guess, glancing at her naked shoulders for the one hundredth time in the last twenty seconds. "Sexy bar girl?"

"What? No. Oh, wait." She grabs something from inside and bends to put it on. When she turns to face me, half her face is covered by a white-and-gold mask with a white peacock feather sticking up on the side.

I can't think of who she's supposed to be, but I can tell by the way she's looking at me that it should be obvious.

"Um . . ."

"Christine. You know. *Phantom of the Opera*."

"Yeah. Right. You look just like her."

"You have no idea who I'm talking about, do you?"

"Not really. I mean, I've heard of it, but I don't know the story."

She rolls her eyes and smiles. "Come on in."

"You should probably make a list of movies you'd like me to see. You know, so we can avoid your general disappointment," I say.

Callie laughs.

We head to her room, and for a moment I entertain the

fantasy that we are together and we're going upstairs to make out. That illusion is shattered when she points to the chair in front of her makeup mirror.

"Sit, please."

"What are you—"

"Don't be scared."

"I'm not scared." I'm curious because she's all hyped up and I have no idea why. What is Callie planning to do with me?

She points to a black hat, cane, and black cloak spread out on her bed. "This is for you."

"What is it?"

"The Phantom's cape. But we have to get you ready first."

"You mean I'm supposed to wear those over what I've got on?"

"Of course. This costume only works if we're both dressed up."

Callie opens her makeup kit and uses a wedge to start applying a light sand color to my face. It tickles and makes me sneeze right away.

"Sorry," I say.

"It's okay. I actually sneeze too when I put this stuff on. But don't worry. It'll come off real easy when we're all done."

Callie bends close to my face as if to study her canvas. Her breathing is soft and steady like a summer breeze on my cheeks. Her blouse is open and reveals the slight line of her cleavage. I imprint the image in my mind so that I can draw her later. I imagine my hand running along the line, shading in the curve of her breast underneath her top. A flush rises in my face and I shift in my chair, hoping she can't tell how she's making me feel.

"You okay?"

"Yeah, sure." I drop my gaze.

"Your cheeks are a little red. Don't be nervous."

"I'm not." I stare at her.

"Close your eyes."

I do and she applies makeup around them. I imagine reaching for her, pulling her close to me. Her lips are almost on mine when she starts talking.

"Now, the Phantom is very handsome, but he was in a tragic fire years ago. Half of his face is normal; the other half is disfigured. The ugly part will be covered by a mask, but I have to make your mouth droop a bit underneath." She touches the bottom half of my lip and my body trembles. I hold the sides of the chair with both of my hands. I stare straight ahead, trying not to look into her eyes.

When she's done, she turns me to face the mirror. I look just like she described. Dark circles encase my eyes. One half of my face looks like it's melting. My bottom lip is swollen like it's spilling down my face. Even my eyebrows droop. The other side of my face is normal, except my skin is now a pasty pale color.

"You've turned my face into a living Dalí portrait," I say.

"Exactly," she says. "See, that's why you're so cool, Neruda. What other guy would know about Dalí? I like him with all his melting watches and trees."

She holds the bottom of my chin with her hand and turns me this way and that as she checks her work.

"Not bad, Callie. Not bad at all," she says.

I may not look attractive, but it's definitely the look she was going for. Maybe it's even a face she can imagine kissing.

She begins to loosely touch my arms, my chest, and my neck as she helps me with the costume. She places the black fedora on top of my head, then ties the cape around my neck and hands me the cane. I stand in front of the floor-length mirror on her wall.

"Ta-da!" she says.

A smile plays grotesquely across my mouth. The cape. The hat. The cane. I am the Phantom, but I'm also some twisted version of The Poet when he was young. It's a little unnerving.

Women beware of the power of his words, because your fall will be swift and all-consuming.

Forget women. All I need tonight is one particular girl to fall for me.

Callie stands at my side and I touch the edge of her dress. Even though she's a tiny bit taller than me in her heels, we look like we belong together.

"Oh. One last thing," she says.

She places a white mask over the half of my face that's distorted.

"Now you're perfect."

Downstairs we pose for pictures like we're going to the prom or something. Callie's mom directs us in all of these overly dramatic positions.

Callie turns away from me and I grab her arm as if I'm pulling her back.

Click.

Callie is on the floor, clutching my leg, and I look down at her menacingly.

Click.

In the last shot, I stand behind Callie, holding her neck with one hand as she leans back into me. My other hand encircles her waist.

Click.

Callie waves good-bye to her parents as we pull away from the curb. Then she finally does what I've been hoping she would: She wraps her arms around my waist.

I don't care where we go. I don't care what we do. I don't care that I look like a psycho. I don't care about anything except how it feels to have her arms wrapped around me and how her body molds against mine with each turn.

Callie directs me from behind, and our destination, the

Walt Disney Concert Hall downtown, comes way too soon. I could have ridden with her forever.

"What're we doing here?" I ask.

"Going to the movies."

Of course we are.

She points up to a sign that says LA PHIL PRESENTS PHANTOM OF THE OPERA.

We get quite the attention at the will call booth. People think we're part of the experience or something and ask us to pose for pictures with them. It's like we're those superhero characters along Hollywood Boulevard by the Grauman's Chinese Theatre. Callie acts all coy, as if she's both attracted and repulsed by me. I give the cape a flourish like I'm a matador and she's the bull. One couple actually gives us five dollars.

Inside the theater, I notice most of the people in the audience are much older and dressed in really nice clothes. We are the only ones in character, and we get more than a few stares as we find our seats. Normally this would embarrass me, but the mask helps. No one here would recognize the real me if I passed them on the street.

The lights go out as the curtain opens and the low, menacing tones of a live orchestra play while the title credits roll in black and white on a huge screen.

Callie leans in and whispers, "With old movies, they always

showed all the credits in the beginning." It sends shivers along my spine.

The movie opens on a guy walking around a dungeon with an old lantern. He doesn't find what he's looking for, and the next scene switches to the Paris Opera House, where they're putting on some sort of ballet.

Even though it's slow, in black and white, and there's no talking, I'm drawn in by the live music. It kind of reminds me of the Hollywood Bowl and when they do the John Williams experience, where the orchestra plays music from all of his movies while scenes from them play on the huge screen. From what I can tell, Christine is an up-and-coming singer and a man named Raoul wants to marry her, but she wants to have a career. The Phantom, who lives at the opera house and watches Christine from one of the boxes each night, is also in love with her and has murdered people so that she can become the star.

We sit there in the dark, not even an armrest separating us. Callie's hands are folded in her lap. I keep stealing glances at them, trying to work up the nerve to touch them. The closest I get is to place my arm down between us. We are now shoulder to shoulder and she doesn't scoot away. We must be glued together because I suddenly find I can't move. I can barely breathe.

When the Phantom's face is revealed, it looks nothing like the makeup that Callie did for me. This Phantom has a pig nose—his nostrils are large and black. His face is a living skeleton.

The end of the movie has some crazy action scene with kidnapping and death and near drowning, and an angry mob eventually kills the Phantom. Christine marries Raoul and lives happily ever after.

We stand with the audience and applaud the philharmonic.

"So, what'd you think?" Callie asks.

"I'm glad you didn't make me up to look like him."

"Yeah, I like the musical Phantom makeup better. It's a more romanticized version of the story. But what's interesting about this movie is that the actor who played the Phantom came up with his own makeup. He was also the guy who did the original *Hunchback of Notre Dame*."

"Cool." I make a mental note to watch *The Hunchback of Notre Dame*.

We walk through the halls and exit through the large doors to the outside.

"Another fun fact of the night for you," she says. "When the Phantom's face was revealed for live audiences, supposedly women shrieked and even fainted. It was pretty scary for its time." She giggles and hugs herself.

The night air is cooler now than when we entered the theater. I take off my cape and wrap it around Callie with a dramatic flair.

"Why, thank you, sir." She curtsies.

"You're welcome, m'lady." I bow in her direction.

Suddenly, I feel bold in my costume, so I touch Callie's corset. "I didn't notice Christine in one of these either."

She shrugs. "Artistic embellishment."

"You're a better Christine than the movie version."

"Thanks," she says. "It's fun being someone else, if only for a little while, don't you think?"

"Sometimes."

"You can stop worrying about things and kind of hide a little from it all, know what I mean?"

I nod, realizing I haven't thought about my family and the drama with my parents all night. I've been able to be a different person—one who is twisted and powerful and in love with Christine. It feels nice.

The streetlights have come on now, and it feels much later than it really is. Callie's looking up at me, and I get that idea about kissing her again.

Suddenly she bends down and removes her shoes.

"I can't wear these for another minute. They are so uncomfortable."

"Why'd you wear them?"

"Because they look good with the outfit."

"You should have worn your boots."

"I almost did, but that wouldn't have been authentic to Christine."

She walks alongside me, heels in one hand, the other holding the black cape to her chest. Our steps barely make a sound.

"Be careful you don't step on glass or anything."

She looks at the ground. "You think there's glass?"

"We're downtown on a dirty street, there could be anything. Hope you've had your tetanus shot."

That makes her stop.

"Here," I say, and hold my arms out in front of her.

"What are you doing?"

"Giving you a lift."

"I'm fine. It's not that far of a walk."

"Come on. I don't want you getting tetanus on my conscience."

"I got my shot this year."

I pick her up and stumble a bit. I try to hide it by swaying side to side and making an airplane noise like she's a kid.

She laughs. "I'm too heavy."

"No you're not."

She giggles close to my ear, and my whole body buzzes.

"You're crazy," she says.

"Says the girl who dresses up like old movie characters."

"You did too!" She's laughing harder now and buries her face in my neck. "Only by force."

"Only by force," I repeat, and carry her all the way back to my scooter with a smile plastered on my face.

. . .

When we get to Callie's house, I walk her up to the front door. The outside light is on, but it casts more of a glow than a bright beam.

Callie turns toward me and I can feel it. This is my moment. She laughs.

If there's anything that annihilates my nerve, it's Callie cracking up at me a split second before I'm about to kiss her. I back away from her instead.

"You've got to see your face," she says.

She takes out a compact from her purse. At some point, the makeup had started to smear, or maybe I smeared it with my hand, and now I look like I've let some little kid color with crayon all over my face. I'm a sad, demented clown. I laugh too, trying to save face.

"Thanks for coming with me," she says. "And for helping me avoid tetanus."

She comes toward me and gives me a hug. It's not a pat-on-the-back, side kind of hug. It's a real, full hug. I let my head fall on her shoulder and feel her body absorb mine as if we are a perfect fit. I smell her hair and feel her cheek against my own.

Everything slows down. I feel her heart beating. Or maybe it's mine. We're so close, I can't tell.

All I know is that there won't be another moment more perfect than this.

I turn my face toward Callie and kiss her.

My entire body tingles with excitement and energy.

I've imagined this moment a thousand times. I have tasted her lips in my dreams. It feels like the earth is shifting and the stars are exploding—the way they do in my mind.

Then I realize. Her body is tense, her glossy lips are stiff.

I pull back and see that her eyes are wide and dark.

I drop my gaze and stare at a crack in the concrete. I watch as the crack becomes a jagged scar, providing a newfound clarity, a certain truth that now lies like a wide fissure between us. I feel a slight chill in the air.

"Neruda," she starts to say, pulling the cape tighter around her body.

"Sorry," I say.

I stumble away from the door and the light, my heart bleeding with each step, thankful when I reach the dark of the street and my bike. My chest feels heavy and it's suddenly hard to breathe. Everything I ever learned about love from The Poet swarms me like bees wakened from their hive. The passion and the joy, the cruel ache that has grabbed hold of me. The knowledge of that gap in my soul. My head swells with all the buzzing. I hold my chest and feel the pain tightening around my heart.

SHORE OF THE HEART

The next day, I wait for Ezra at our designated meeting spot—
Union Station underneath the *City of Dreams/River of History*
mural. It's this iconic mural containing huge portraits of the
people of LA, from the original Native Americans to contem-
porary Angelenos.

I take a couple of pictures for reference, not that the mu-
ral Luis and I are working on will look anything like this one.
I'm not as talented as this artist, but it's good for perspective.
I love the color of it all against the striking blue background.
The different shades of brown on the faces. I look up the spe-
cifics on this mural; it's twenty-five by eighty feet. I wonder if

I'd be able to do a mural this large in scope someday.

Ezra finds me as I'm making notes in my phone.

"Hey, man." He's carrying a huge backpack.

"You look like you're going to scale a mountain," I say.

"That's the plan."

"Really? Because I don't think I'll make it with this." I refer to my bulky school backpack and sleeping bag. Ezra said I only needed a change of clothes. He didn't say anything about hiking.

"Not this weekend, but in the future."

"Oh," I say. I wonder where we'd go. Maybe we could take one of those backpacking trips around Europe, sleep in hostels, meet European girls. Maybe I'd have more luck with love in another country.

As Ezra and I walk to the train, a brown-haired girl crosses my peripheral vision. I snap my head in her direction.

It isn't Callie.

I've done that three times already. Every girl looks like Callie today. She haunts me. Trailing me like some broken promise.

Was it only just last night that I had the best and worst night of my life? Where Callie and I began and ended in one half-lit moment on her porch?

I check my phone. A compulsion, an instinct I can't seem to shake.

There's no text from Callie. Not that I expect one. Part of me wonders if I'll ever hear from her again. I certainly haven't tried contacting her.

Thankfully, it's the weekend. Hopefully Ezra won't ask me about Callie. Hopefully I can go a day without thinking about her. So far I haven't been able to go five minutes without seeing the way her eyes looked after I kissed her. How surprised and sad they were at the same time.

And I can't help but wonder if I know anything at all about love. If it's possible to have a love that is lasting and true. More important, I wonder if love is real, or if it's this elusive thing that might always be just out of reach.

"Ready?" Ezra asks, bringing me back to the present.

"Ready," I say. I shake off thoughts of Callie, pick up my stuff, and follow Ezra's lead.

The train isn't crowded, so we grab a four-seater and settle in for the ride. Ezra takes out a book and begins reading *The Autobiography of Malcolm X*.

"How is it?" I ask Ezra.

"Really good, man. I'm still in the early years. Did you know he went to prison too?"

"Because of civil disobedience?"

"No, it was before all that. When he was Malcolm Little."

Ezra looks out the window. The blinding morning light

reflects off the ocean, making it a huge blue mirror as we speed past. The sky is cloudless.

"In prison, you become obsessed with time. You count days, hours, weeks. You fill time with whatever you can. You work out. You read. You take classes. You have to do something. Because you're suddenly aware of time and how it takes up everything. How it presses in on you from every side and there's no escaping it because it's all you have."

"What happens with the time when you get out?" I ask.

He sighs. "You try to get it back, but you realize it's impossible."

"Do you ever wish you could? Just go back to that night and undo everything, I mean?"

Ezra stares at me as if he's looking past me or through me to someplace deep in memory.

"Nah. The only thing you can do is try to focus on the time you have left, think about the future."

He drops his gaze back to his book.

If I could time travel, I'd go back to Friday night and never kiss Callie.

No, I'd travel back to that day in Mr. Nelson's class. I'd remove my name from the coffee can so that when Callie reached her hand inside, she couldn't pull mine out. We'd never be partners. We'd never become friends. I'd never fall in love with her or feel her rejection.

And I'd never know the feel of her lips, so still, against mine.

We get off the train in Goleta, a city just north of Santa Barbara, where the campground is. The train station is more like a dock with an overhang. Lots of college-aged people with bikes get off and speed away. UCSB must be close.

Ezra sniffs at the air. "Smell that?"

"What?"

"The ocean."

He's right. The air is cleaner and crisper here, almost as if we're at a higher elevation. There's just the slightest bit of chill. Ezra wraps a scarf around his neck.

We walk to the campsite, which spreads out across the top of a cliff overlooking the ocean and meanders down a hill and up against the sand. Even though it's November, the place is packed with RVs and dotted with tents of all sizes and shapes and colors.

We check in and find our site covered in shade beneath two tall palms, set close to the sand. It's away from most of the RVs and other campers. A couple of kids play in the distance behind some ferns and bushes, and a dog barks out of sight.

I help Ezra set up a tiny orange tent.

"Where do I sleep?"

"In here," he says.

I open the flap and peek inside.

"You sure it's big enough for both of us?"

"Definitely, man. It'll look bigger once you set up your stuff."

Our sleeping bags fit side by side, just barely, but it'll work. There's pretty much room to sleep and sit up, that's it.

"Kind of small," I say.

"It's a tent."

"Yeah, well, you should see what my parents call a tent."

"Oh yeah?"

"They have one with three compartments, and my mom brings a huge blow-up bed that she decorates with pillows. She even puts a flowered welcome mat at the entrance."

"You're kidding."

"Nope."

"That's a whole other level of camping."

"Yeah," I say.

But I don't want to think about my parents. I'm annoyed with myself for bringing them up. I change the subject quickly.

"So, um, what's the deal for dinner?" I ask.

I look around and don't see a cooler.

"I figured we could buy stuff up here to make," Ezra says. "There's a market somewhere on the grounds. I brought some protein bars though, if you want one."

I nod and he tosses me a peanut butter one. Then we decide to explore the grounds a bit. We walk down a narrow path that weaves in and out of green bushes and make our way to the beach. To our right is the coastline, covered with rolling hills that end at the water in cliffs. To the left is more beach and Santa Barbara.

The sand is filled with small clusters of people sitting in beach chairs or on blankets. There's an abandoned blue lifeguard tower.

We take off our shoes and socks and leave them on the beach, then roll up the bottoms of our jeans and step into the water.

I immediately jump back. It's super cold.

Ezra stays planted in place and lets the water break over him. The waves rush up to the middle of his calves.

"It's not that bad," he tells me.

"Yes, it is that bad."

But I keep him company anyway.

For a long time we just watch the water as it comes and goes. Then Ezra removes his hat and shirt.

"Come on," he says.

"You're going in? You're crazy."

"Yeah, man. It's perfect."

"Without your shorts?"

"Already wearing them." He drops his jeans and, sure enough, he's got a red bathing suit on.

I don't really want to go in, but I decide that in this moment I don't have to be me. I can be someone who sees the ocean and doesn't think of love and loss. I can be someone who feels alive in the rush of its waters instead.

I run back up to our tent and put on my suit. By the time I return to the beach, Ezra is pretty far out.

There's only one way to do this. I take a long breath and yell and rush into the water. The ocean is ice breaking against my skin, but I smash through it and dive into a wave. My ears burn as I break through the surface.

"It's freezing!" I yell, and swim over to Ezra.

He laughs. "But you're alive! Isn't it amazing? Here comes one."

A large wave rolls toward us. Ezra swims out a little ahead of it and throws his body forward in a dive, but he gets taken under and is tossed around. He comes up for air and shakes his head to get the water and hair out of his face.

"So close," I tell him.

"I haven't bodysurfed in years, man. I think I forgot how. You ever try it?"

I nod and show him a few tips that I picked up from my dad when I was younger.

The waves are a good size, not too big, and Ezra catches more waves than he misses.

After a while I'm either too numb to feel anything or my body has gotten used to the temperature. I glance back at the shore. Our shoes look tiny, like remnants of small people whose bodies have been ripped away from them.

We swim until we're both exhausted. Then we sit on the

sand, towels wrapped around our skin, watching the water.

"This is perfect," Ezra says.

"Yeah," I agree. Here there's no parents, no Callie, no problems. It's only Ezra and me.

We stay that way, like two Buddhas planted in the sand, our shadows shifting with the sun until it has set.

Later that night, we head to the market and pick up everything we need for dinner tonight and tomorrow's breakfast.

Ezra makes a fire and cooks the hamburgers on the grill rack. We eat in silence, each absorbed in our own thoughts. I've been trying not to think about Callie, but she keeps worming her way into my head. I keep seeing the way she looked after I kissed her, the shock and unexpectedness of that kiss. Like she'd rather be anywhere but there with me.

I finish the burger with tears in my eyes and look away so Ezra doesn't see.

We spend the rest of the evening reading by the fire. I've decided to give The Poet another chance, but his words are raw, more visceral than ever before. I struggle through them and read from his biography too, hoping to understand the man behind the words a little more.

I'm surprised to learn that at the end of his life The Poet had cancer, but he was supposedly doing well, maybe even in remission. Then there was that military coup in Chile. Since The Poet was an influential, outspoken member of the Chilean Communist Party, he was a target of the new dictatorship. He was actually supposed to flee to Mexico because the Mexican ambassador offered him safe passage. But only twelve days after Augusto Pinochet's military coup, The Poet suddenly died.

"Do you think Neruda was poisoned?" I ask Ezra.

He's got a small notebook he writes in every now and then; he pauses from his writing to look up. "Didn't they exhume his body and find he died of natural causes?" Ezra asks.

"Yeah, but . . . it still seems kind of suspicious, don't you think? Maybe one of the many women he wronged killed him."

"Well, look who's jaded now."

I pick at a thread hanging from my shirt.

"The simplest answer is usually correct. Occam's razor and all," Ezra says.

"Oh." I pretend like I know what Occam's razor is.

"Hey, did you know Malcolm X taught himself to read in prison?" he asks.

"Really?"

"He started with the dictionary. He copied every word and definition by hand because he couldn't read and understand the books he wanted to. He spent as many hours a day he could studying and reading. He taught himself history and philosophy and psychology. He said he was actually grateful for the time he spent in prison. It changed his life. If there ever was an argument for educating those in the prison system, this is it, man. He was brilliant. But he was also angry. Too bad his anger fueled everything."

Listening to Ezra talk makes me wonder if there's a part of him that feels grateful for his time in prison as well.

I put another log on the fire.

"So . . . what's the plan?" I ask.

"Hmm?" Ezra keeps his eyes on his book.

"The plan. I mean, I assume we're here for a reason."

"We're camping, man. That's the reason."

"Yeah, but . . . we're in Santa Barbara. You're trying to tell me that's just a coincidence?"

Ezra closes his book and sets it down in the dirt. He pokes the burning wood, nudging the embers with a stick. They brighten to orange and quickly fade. I wait for him to speak.

"I'm meeting Daisy tomorrow for lunch."

"I knew it. Seriously?"

"Yeah."

"You just called her up?"

"Yeah."

Ezra keeps messing with the fire. Half of his face is covered in shadow.

"Awesome," I say.

"We'll see."

"No, it'll be good. You'll see her, she'll see you, and it'll be just like old times. You guys are meant to be."

"We'll see," he says again.

I'm happy for Ezra. If I can't have love, at least he should be able to.

He faces the fire again. But out of the corner of my eye, I see his mouth turned upward in a smile.

IF YOU FORGET ME

In the morning, I wake up all stiff, but it's hard to tell if it's from sleeping on a slope and a rock, or from tossing and turning to escape the thoughts of Callie that pursued me all night. The more I think of her, the more it hurts. I've fallen for girls before, been disappointed, but it's never felt like this. It's never felt like someone has ripped my heart out, backed over it multiple times with a semi truck so that it's all mangled and torn, and then shoved it back inside my chest. It's only been two days, but it feels like I've carried this hurt for months.

If this is love, how do people stand it? And how do they manage to do it over and over again?

I turn over and realize that Ezra is already gone.

I can feel the chill of the morning air inside the tent, so I go outside and make another fire and some coffee. I have a banana and some almonds for breakfast.

I look around for Ezra, but I can't find him, so I walk down to the shore. The beach is completely deserted. My footprints are the only ones that mark the sand as far as I can see. I breathe in the sea air deeply. I take out my sketchbook and start drawing the gray ocean.

A while later, Ezra plops down next to me.

"Where'd you go?"

"Early hike."

"I would have come."

"I didn't want to wake you." He takes off his beanie and shakes out his hair. "Let me see what you've got."

I show him my drawing.

"That's great, man. I don't know how you do that."

"Lots of practice."

"It's not just about the practice. It's the way you see things. You see what others don't. I'm not sure you can practice that. It's a gift."

I nudge him and he pushes me back, and soon we're both on our feet, trying to take the other down.

Ezra is supposed to meet Daisy at a restaurant on State Street over in the heart of Santa Barbara. The bus lets us out on a street that's like an open-air mall filled with all kinds of stores from furniture to clothing to antiques and jewelry.

Small brick walkways curve around buildings. The place has an old Spanish feel to it. Trees in small patches of earth, protected by black wrought iron circles, are planted equidistantly along both sides of the street. It's all very clean. No wrappers or plastic bags or cigarette butts on the ground. No graffiti climbing up walls. But there is a surprisingly large number of homeless men and women here that reminds me of the Santa Monica Pier.

When we arrive at the intersection across from the restaurant, Ezra hesitates. Through the window, I see what looks like a group of people in the center. In the front corner, there's a woman with dark hair sitting by herself. It's got to be Daisy. Ezra looks over his shoulder like he's thinking about turning back.

"Want me to go with you?" I ask.

"No." Ezra stares straight ahead, but he doesn't move forward. "We'll meet up afterward? I'll text you."

"No problem. Go do your thing."

Ezra pulls himself up straighter.

"Good luck," I say.

"Thanks." He crosses the street.

I sit at one of the outdoor tables of another restaurant. It's got large green bushes in wooden boxes to shield the ongoing traffic and pedestrians, but I can still see Daisy, or who I think is Daisy, from where I'm positioned.

Ezra enters the restaurant just as a waiter brings me a menu and asks if I'd like anything to drink.

"Thai iced tea," I say.

I check my phone for a message from Callie.

Nothing. Only a text from Greyson wanting to know where I'm at.

Across the way, I watch Daisy and Ezra like they're in a silent movie. Daisy stands up as Ezra approaches her. She smiles and gives him a hug. They embrace. He's all smiles. They sit down, look at a menu.

What will they say after the hellos and the how-are-yous and the "hey, you look great after all these years"? Has her heart ached for him too?

Daisy reaches across the table and places her hand on Ezra's. She says something to him, but I can't make out what they're saying.

I order the green chili rice with chicken when the waiter returns. Then I open my sketchbook and begin drawing a pair of eyes the color of sand.

WALKING AROUND

Down by the ocean, the air is crisp and salty. Ezra and I face the crashing waves that roll and retreat along the shore. A couple walks by holding hands, nodding in our direction as they pass.

Three gray birds peck at the sand in front of us and sprint along the shoreline every time the tide comes in.

Ezra is silent, just as he's been since I met him at the intersection after his lunch with Daisy. I want to ask him what happened, but it's clear he doesn't want to talk about it.

Finally he says, "She's still so beautiful . . ."

He stares ahead at the open sea.

"But she's different. I'm different. And it's not just that

we look a little older. Ten years is an eternity. Sitting across from her, I thought it'd be more like a time machine. Like we'd travel back to when we were kids, which is crazy, I know, man. But . . . you can never go back." He turns and looks at me and the harsh midday light exposes the lines on his face.

"But what'd she say?"

"She said all the right things. That she was so happy to see me. That I looked good. But there was an uneasiness, a sadness in her eyes that was never there before." Ezra digs the toe of his shoe into the sand. "It was stupid to look her up."

"Is she married or anything?"

"No."

"Is she in a relationship?"

"No."

"So she's available, then."

"No," he says.

"I don't understand."

"Listen, Neruda, sometimes you miss your window. The feelings hang on like old ghosts, but they're not real. Daisy and I ended the moment I made that stupid decision to rob someone's house. The day I tried to save Rafa, I lost everything. I kind of knew that already, but seeing Daisy . . . it all became clear. I can't keep living in the past."

"But . . ." I want to say that there are things worth fighting for. That love should be one of those things we hold on to and

252

only let go of when life gives us no other choice. Instead, I say, "But she was the one."

Ezra shakes his head. "I don't even know what that means, man. 'The one.' Maybe instead of looking for the one, we should just work on our own shit. Become our best self and then, you know, choose someone to love and be good to that person."

"Yeah, but . . . what if the person you choose doesn't choose you back?" I ask, my voice as small as one of the birds pecking the sand.

"I don't know," he says. "But being here with nature all around, a good friend by my side . . . You can't ask for much more than that."

This can't be right. The day is not working out at all like I thought it would. The sky darkens and the ocean becomes a sad wet thing. I zip up my jacket.

"What did you say to her?"

"I told her good-bye."

I kick at the sand.

"You're going to be okay, Neruda. Whatever happens with your parents, the girl, school, your art, even this punk kid Luis. You're going to be okay. I want you to remember that."

"Whatever."

"Come on, say 'I'm going to be okay.'" Ezra nudges me with his shoulder, but my feet slip a little into the sand.

"I'm going to be okay," I say, my voice flat like paper.

"I'm going to be okay," he repeats softly, and then again, like the pulsing tide, until the ocean itself is telling us so.

It takes us half the time to pack up our site as when we set it up. Ezra is quieter than usual, and I am too. Everything has changed.

We walk back up to the small Goleta station and wait for our train.

"Thanks for coming with me," Ezra says. "Sorry if it's been a downer."

"No, it was good," I say, which isn't true and he knows it.

"We didn't even talk about what's going on with you."

"Nothing's going on," I say. Unfortunately this is all true. There is nothing going on between me and Callie.

"I'm sorry, man." He gives me a look that says he understands. Then he says, "So, um, I need to tell you something, but you're not going to like it."

I look at Ezra, worried about what that's supposed to mean. But seeing him there with his huge pack, something clicks. I know what he's going to tell me before he says it.

"You're not coming home," I say.

He shakes his head. "I should have told you earlier, but . . ."

"You wanted to see how it went with Daisy first?"

"Kind of. Maybe, man. I don't know what I'm doing. All I know is that I've been stuck in the same spot for years. I've got to get moving and keep moving."

I nod my head. "Where are you gonna go?"

"I don't know." He laughs nervously. "Maybe just pick a random spot on a map or something. Am I crazy?"

"No. No, I get it."

But there's a tightness in my chest. I focus on the schedule that's taped up on the wall because I don't want to get too emotional.

The train comes in. Ezra takes off his pack and pulls me in for a hug.

"I'm going to miss you, bro," he says. "Onward and upward, my man. Onward and upward."

He pats me on the back twice and lets me go. There are tears in both our eyes. I get on the train and take a window seat. Before the train pulls away, I look back to the platform.

Ezra is sitting on a bench, pack next to him, his book already open, his head bent over, reading. He glances up at me when the train starts to pull away. He holds up his hand in a final good-bye, and I keep my eyes focused on the scenery until it all becomes a blur.

TONIGHT I CAN WRITE
THE SADDEST LINES

On the ride home, I stare out the window as the meaning behind the empty seat across from me gradually sinks in. Ezra is gone; who knows when I'll see him again. Maybe never.

And maybe he's right, that you can't live in the past, but I still don't understand. I don't understand why he couldn't have just chosen Daisy. Or why Dad had to cheat on Mom. Why Callie doesn't want me.

I look around at the train car. It's full of people. But I am completely alone.

I check my phone for a text like I've been doing for the past two days.

Nothing.

Maybe I could just reach out to Callie, act like it was no big deal. I start to type *Hi*, but I delete it. What's there to say to her?

I open the worn pages of Neruda's *Twenty Love Songs* and turn right to "The Song of Despair." I've read it many times. But now I understand the shipwreck of his soul and the debris and the cold, cold death of his love's kisses. How she became dangerous and how he sank. How she sank him. She abandoned him and he was left drowning in sorrow. In the end, he's just standing on the shore alone, deserted like an empty harbor.

Is this how all love begins and ends? In the quiet torment of the soul? If this is what it's like to love, I don't ever want to love someone again.

I close the book and put my earbuds in. I find the radio program *Lovesongs on the Coast* because as long as I'm miserable, I might as well excel at it. I listen to Jules, who says that she can't imagine her life without Robbie. He's everything to her and she wants him to know that she's thinking of him tonight. She requests "I Will Always Love You," the country version by Dolly Parton.

I hate country music, but by the second verse my eyes are all watery. Again. I turn away from the other passengers so they won't see me.

It's hard to hear other people talk about their supreme happiness, but there's something cathartic about listening to the calls that come in about the loves people have lost. That pain matches my own and, at least for the moment, it's like there's someone out there who gets me.

The more I listen, the more the love songs become a soundtrack, and I play a montage of scenes in my mind. When Callie and I were paired up and I first noticed her eyes. When she invited me over and touched my face. When I drew her on that perfect day at LACMA, and she blushed. When we sat together at the movies and then I carried her to my scooter. When she wrapped her arms around me on the back of my bike.

The images and love songs are like salt in a wound, but I don't care.

I want to hurt.

When I get home, my parents are on the couch. The soundtrack of *Man of La Mancha* plays in the background. Mom breaks from Dad like a piece in a jigsaw puzzle and stands to greet me.

"Welcome home!" she says. "How was camping?"

"Fine," I say. I drop my pack and sleeping bag. They hit the floor with a loud thud.

"We missed you. Dad's been torturing me with his old music."

"This is not torture. Listen, this is about true love. The passion for his *amor*." He holds out his hand toward Mom and begins serenading her with "Dulcinea." He gets up, saunters toward her, and pulls her into his arms for a dance. "Dulcinea . . . I see heaven when I see thee . . . Dulcinea."

"Carlos . . ."

Dad ignores her pleas and spins her around the living room, still singing. Mom's laughing. But something within me snaps, because it's all a huge lie.

It's broken.

Everything is broken.

There is no true love, no such thing as soul mates. There's only loving and leaving.

I stop the music.

"Dad, don't you think there's something you should tell Mom?"

Dad's wide grin freezes. Mom looks at him, at me, and then back at him. His eyes plead with me like a trapped animal. Mom must feel the change in the air, because she backs away from Dad.

"What's wrong?" Mom asks.

"Nothing," Dad says. "Nothing's wrong."

"He's lying. Everything's wrong," I say.

Mom looks from me to Dad again, and now there's real worry on her face.

Dad turns to me. "Neruda, let's go for a walk."

"No, Dad. Mom should know."

"What should I know?"

"Come on," Dad says, and he grabs my arm hard and shoves me toward the door.

"Tell her about Leslie," I say loudly.

Dad opens the door and pushes me out of it, but Mom is right behind, and all three of us stumble onto the front porch. Dad still hasn't replaced the bulb, so we're in the dark with only a little light spilling outside from the living room, creating menacing shadows along the wall of the house.

"Carlos, what are you doing?"

"Tell her," I say louder.

Dad's eyes are wild now, panicked. He's looking everywhere but at Mom's face.

"*Ahuevonado,*" Dad spits out, and turns to Mom. "It's nothing, Janice. Nothing. Neruda's blowing something way out of proportion."

"Tell her," I say.

Dad glances across the street as if he's thinking about making a run for it. Instead, he faces Mom. "Janice, you know that I love you—"

And that just sets me off.

"He cheated, Mom. He cheated. With a girl named Leslie."

I can't help it; the words just fall out of my mouth. But the second they're out, I regret saying them.

Mom reaches back for the wall to steady herself.

My voice rises the more I speak. "And I found out, and he didn't want me to tell you, but I can't walk around here like I don't know anymore. It's all wrong. Everything is wrong."

"Neruda, calm down," Dad says.

"Mom doesn't deserve this. I don't deserve this."

"Who's Leslie?" Mom asks.

"His TA. She's like twenty-one or something."

"Oh, Carlos." My mom's voice is more of a groan. "When?"

Dad doesn't even try to deny it, just says, "Last year." He stares at the ground.

"When?"

"I don't know the dates—about a year ago."

"Well, when? Was it the summer, or over Christmas? I'd like to know when you decided your marriage didn't matter and when you were off screwing some girl. Oh!" Her hand goes to her mouth. "You didn't bring her here, did you? Did you?"

"Janice," Dad says.

Mom bends her head and whispers, "Oh God."

"I ended it. It's over and I haven't even thought of her. It was—it was stupid. The second I realized just how dumb I was, I ended it. *Te amo.*"

She holds up a hand like she does when she's angry, but instead of speaking, she starts crying. This makes me afraid, because my mom never cries.

Dad starts crying too.

"No . . . you don't get to do that," she says to him.

"I'm sorry, Janice. I'm so sorry." He sits down on the front steps and puts his head in his hands.

I stand there between them, more sad and scared than angry, because I don't know what happens next.

Mom stares at him and then goes inside, leaving Dad and me on the porch. Neither of us moves to follow her. Dad's shoulders shake from the emotion, but I don't have sympathy for him. He took something from Mom, and something from me too. He took something I thought was real and destroyed it.

I go in the house, grab my bag, and head for my room. When I get there, I slam the door shut. Then I take The Poet's book out of my back pocket and throw it against the wall. It falls to the ground like a wounded bird.

I don't have the heart for his words anymore.

SAD SONG TO
BORE EVERYONE

In the morning, I pretend that I don't notice the sheets and blankets folded on the corner of the living room couch. I also pretend I have something going on before school so that I can leave the house early and avoid my parents. Not that they're trying to find me. Mom hasn't left her room since last night, and Dad is already gone.

I stop at the coffee shop and get some coffee and *pan dulce* and sit on the curb, watching people. When I'm done, I leave the empty cup in the gutter and head for school because I have nowhere else to go.

Ezra is gone.

Callie is gone, not that I ever really had her to begin with.

When I get to class, I can't make myself focus. I don't want to be here. I don't want to be anywhere. Maybe I could just bail on my life and everyone, like Ezra did. It wouldn't be that hard to pack a bag and drive off. Go all the way to Chile. I could do it. Cross the Mexican border and then head south. I'd be like some modern Che getting in touch with my people.

I could set up at one of those beaches that Papi always told me about. I'd live there, alone, underneath the blue sky and the thick trees of the bordering forest. No one would bother me. I could draw and paint all day. I'd be at peace.

Between first and second period, I run into Callie. Of course. Because when you're trying to avoid someone, you start to see them everywhere. It's like a rule.

"Hi," she says, but she says it all wrong. There's something in her voice, something that wasn't there before Friday night. She looks like she's going to try to say more, but I keep moving. I don't want to hear the words. I already know how she feels.

Later, when I'm in the office, trying to get my schedule changed, I see Callie again. My assigned guidance counselor doesn't understand why I need to change English classes in the middle of the semester, and since I can't explain it beyond not wanting to be in class with Callie, she won't make the change. Besides, the only other English class available is an AP level English course—*Do I think I'm up for the challenge? Yes, ma'am*—and it's full.

When I step out of the guidance counselor's office, Callie is sitting on one of the chairs in the hallway. She's looking down at her phone, so I pretend not to see her, how pretty she looks, and quickly walk the other way.

I try to get a pass from Mr. Fisher to get out of English. I tell him that I need the time to work on the mural. He goes for it, but Mr. Nelson won't agree because there's a test. A test I completely forgot about.

Everyone is against me today.

I wait until after the bell rings to show up to class.

"Neruda, you're late," Mr. Nelson says when I enter.

I keep my head down and drop into my seat. I don't look at anyone at my table, especially not Callie.

And she doesn't look at me. In fact, she acts like she doesn't even notice that I'm there. She stares ahead at Mr. Nelson like she's some straight-A student.

I ignore her right back.

While Mr. Nelson passes out the exam, Callie's oversized gray sweater falls and reveals part of her right shoulder. I ignore that part. I ignore that part so hard that I don't notice the freckles on her shoulder next to her black bra strap either.

Her right elbow rests precariously close to my side of the desk, so I scoot over. The elbow and her shoulder, her crossed legs, her tilted head, the way she holds her pen, I ignore them all.

I try to focus on the test in front of me, but it's impossible because I can hear Callie sitting next to me. Her breathing. The blood pumping from her callous heart. Her cells dying and regenerating. Her eyes blinking, the lashes touching down and lifting gently up again like the wings of hummingbirds.

I barely move the entire period. I've never concentrated in class so hard. But if someone were to ask me what the test questions were, I'd have no idea.

I bolt as soon as the bell rings.

I finally find some peace in the library. When Luis shows up after school, I don't give him the chance to make any crude jokes or say much of anything at all. I put him to work on something easy: completing the installation wall.

He lines up the stencils and sprays black paint on them. He peels them off the wall. The words LOVE IS are in black, bold lettering. They mock me. Why did I have to choose that expression? Why couldn't I have gone with *Before I die . . . ?*

I don't want to know what people think love is. I don't want to know anything about love ever again.

"Lame," Luis says. "Whose idea was this, anyway? Yours?"

"I don't know," I lie.

"Yeah, it was yours."

He starts painting in the lines. I return to work on the

mural, determined to make it amazing. But I'm having trouble concentrating, and all I can hear is Luis's stupid voice in my head.

Lame.

Lame.

Lame.

MELANCHOLY IN THE FAMILIES

I manage to spend two days going through the motions at school avoiding Callie, though that isn't hard, because she's just as weird around me. She hasn't said a word to me after that first hello in the hallway.

I can't tell if she's angry or embarrassed. Either way, she's not speaking to me.

It's probably better this way. A quick end rather than a slow, prolonged death.

I'm able to avoid talking to my parents for the most part. Until tonight. I'm doing some homework when there's a knock on my door.

"I already ate," I call out, hoping that'll deter whoever is there. I'm still not in the mood to talk to either one of them—my mom because of how guilty I feel, my dad because of how angry I am.

The door opens and I see Dad in my peripheral vision. I don't make eye contact.

"Can I speak with you for a minute?"

I nod.

"Your mom and I thought it would be best if I gave her some time."

Behind him, I glimpse two bags on the floor of the hallway.

"Where are you going?"

"Tía Lilia's, just for a couple of days, depending on . . ." He looks at one of my drawings on the wall. "However long it takes for us to work things out."

My dad's sister Lilia lives over on the west side, in Culver City.

"Listen, Neruda. I'm sorry, son. I never should have put you in the position I did. It was completely unfair of me and there's no excuse for it. I hope you can forgive me."

I know he wants me to say that I forgive him, that I can move past it. But I'm not sure I can. I'm certainly not ready to now.

"I hear what you're saying, Dad," I say. "But I just need some time too."

Dad nods. I expect him to leave, but he stands in the doorway, looking at my drawings on the wall.

"I don't remember seeing this one before." He nods to the one of Callie at LACMA.

"It's new."

"I like it."

"Thanks."

"You've always had such a way with images. Papi noticed it first. He would have been proud of you. The artist you've become."

"He wanted me to be a poet."

Dad looks at me in surprise. "You are." He touches Callie's face on the wall. "You just use images."

I look at the drawing and then I look at my hands. How inadequate they feel right now. I don't know why I'm torturing myself with her drawing. Staring at it every night. I had planned to give it to Callie. Now I don't know what to do with it.

I sigh loudly.

Dad continues, "Look, I know you're angry with me, but *sigo siendo tu padre, cachai?*" I'm still your father, understand? He comes over and kisses the top of my head like he's been doing since I was little, then turns to go.

I watch him leave and wonder how everything got so messed up. I wish it could all just go back to the way it was.

I look at Callie's picture again. Then I tear if off the wall.

. . .

A few hours later, I can't handle being in my house anymore—
it feels like something died in there—so I head over to Greyson's.
We play a video game for about thirty minutes before I tell him
about my parents.

"Shit. When?" he asks.

"Last year. He's staying at my tía's now."

It's quiet in his room except for the sound of our guns hitting their marks. I know I've caught him a little off guard, because I take out three of his guys.

"Oh, and Callie?" I continue telling him about my depressing life. "Well, let's just call her number nine."

"As in lucky number nine?"

"No."

I maneuver my guy down a dark hallway and relish a particularly bloody kill.

"Sorry," Greyson eventually says.

"Yeah, well, it is what it is."

There's not really much more he can say, or that anyone
can say. It just sucks. And I feel terrible about how I blurted
out everything to my mom. I'm not sure how to make it right
with her.

"My parents went through something like that last year."

"Your dad cheated?"

"No, but they were fighting and yelling all the time. It was stressful."

"Why didn't you tell me?"

"I don't know," he says. "But the point is, it's better now. They dealt with whatever it was, and they're still together." Here, Greyson pauses the game and looks at me. "So there's hope is what I'm saying."

"Yeah," I say and nod, dropping my eyes.

He presses play and we continue the game.

If only I could be so sure.

LOVE IS

The next morning at school, over the loudspeaker, an announcement is made about the love wall. Students are encouraged to participate by writing their own one-liners about what love means to them.

I have nothing to say on the topic.

During art class, I work on finishing the embracing couple.

Call me a sadist.

As I paint them, I try to channel the passion, the raw emotion that I used to feel before Callie rejected me. It falls flat.

In my painting, the girl's face is hidden, but the guy's eyes can be seen peering over her shoulder. They are closed in a peaceful bliss.

Does art imitate life or does life imitate art? I wonder.

I don't know. I only know that I have seen this image somewhere. I have known this feeling. If only briefly.

Someone taps my shoulder, making me jump.

Luis.

I look at the time.

"You're late," I say.

"So what. I'm getting it done. Your love wall is finished, isn't it?"

It is. And even though I would never admit it out loud, Luis did a good job on it. Probably because I marked it out for him and showed him how to do the stencils. All he had to do was trace straight lines with a ruler and spray-paint the stencil lettering.

He points to my couple. "What the hell happened to them?"

"What?"

"You messed the guy up."

"No I didn't."

"Yeah, he looks like shit now, no offense . . . but whatever, this is your thing. So, what's next?"

Luis is standing there, looking at me like I'm supposed to give him something to do. I don't want to give him anything. He doesn't deserve this task—the responsibility of it or the recognition. He's never taken this assignment seriously and now he's totally insulted me. "No offense"? This is my mural. I don't care what Mr. Nelson says. I don't want Luis working with me anymore. There's only so much I can take here.

"Nothing. You're done."

"It doesn't look done to me."

"Not the mural. I'll finish that on my own. *You* are done."

"You can't do that," Luis says.

"I think I just did."

I turn my back on him and face the mural.

In one swift move, Luis slams me up against the wall, twisting my arm. The side of my cheek smears the guy's face I just spent the last hour working on. I try to get out of Luis's hold, but he's stronger and more skilled. I remain quiet, though; I won't give him the satisfaction of crying out from the pain.

"You're no better than me," he whispers close to my ear before he releases me.

I stay against the wall until I hear him walk out the door. Then I take a cloth and wipe my face. I stare at my mutilated couple. The guy's face is half gone. His eyes bleed and run down the wall.

I grab a brush and get back to work.

When school lets out, I have to stop working on the mural for a bit and cover it up so that people can write on the love wall. I figured the wall would fill up quickly, but as I'm cleaning some brushes, I notice that most people seem hesitant about what to write. Some come in with an idea, but many just look at the wall and talk about it.

After the rush of students has dispersed, I notice Callie hesitating by the library door. I wonder what she's doing here. She's usually at practice.

"So that's the big wall?" she asks, her voice like a fresh scab.

She's backed me into a corner here, literally, so I have to respond to her.

"Yeah. There's chalk, so, you know, feel free."

Callie doesn't move toward the wall. Instead, she leans against the door like she hasn't quite made up her mind about being here. The longer she stays there, the more it starts to irritate me. Either you're in or you're out. There's no halfway.

But she just stands there.

She doesn't speak. She stares at the ground.

"Look, I've got to keep working, so . . ." I make a move toward my brushes and get back to painting.

"I'm sorry I didn't respond the way you wanted that night," she says. Her voice is barely above a whisper, but it cuts through the air between us and I can hear it as if she were standing right next to me. "It's just that I don't want to be in a relationship like that with anyone right now. I thought I knew how you felt, but then I wasn't sure and, anyway, I'm sorry. I never meant to hurt you. I definitely didn't want to lose you as a friend."

There she goes with that word again. I hate that word.

"Whatever. It wasn't a big deal. I don't know why you're even bringing it up. I haven't even thought about it since."

I want her to just go, to just get out of my life because I don't want to be reminded of her, of the pain that's always in my chest and that now rises in my throat.

"You know, the world doesn't revolve around you, Neruda. Other people are going through stuff too. But I guess you're so focused on yourself that you can't even see that."

"What are you talking about?" I turn to face her, and this time I notice that the skin around her eyes is a little blotchy. And even though I don't want it to, my heart aches for her. Because seeing Callie suffering somehow is worse than my own. Part of me wants to run across the room and take her in my arms. I take a small step in her direction, but her eyes stop me. They are a distant gray. They tell me I am a boat marooned on a shore, cut off from the water.

"Nothing," she says. "Good luck with your mural. See you around."

She's out the door before I can say anything else.

I try to shake off the exchange with Callie and focus on the embracing couple. They need more work, but there's something missing from the overall piece too. I step away from the mural. It's like I need another piece to fill the space. But I don't know what that image should be.

I decide to take a break. I'll think about it tonight and come back to the wall tomorrow when I have a fresh perspective.

I glance over at the art installation wall and read a couple of the responses:

Love is being totally comfortable around someone

Love is LIKE A PUPPY ALL HAPPY TO SEE YOU

Love is chocolate

Love is a choice

Love is BELIEVING the BEST ABOUT A PERSON

Love is being there when someone needs you

I pick up a piece of blue chalk and complete the phrase with a word of my own.

Love is overrated

ALMOST OUT OF THE SKY

When I get home, there's a letter from Ezra waiting for me on the kitchen table. I grab a bag of chips and a drink and head upstairs to my room. I feel a twinge of nostalgia as I open his letter. It reminds me of when he was in prison and we wrote real letters to each other. Everything seemed much easier then.

Dear Neruda,
    By now I will have left after our trip to Santa Barbara. I'm sorry, but I was afraid if I didn't go, I'd never leave. Fear has defined me for too long. I'm tired of being

afraid of life, of the past, of not having a future.

If there's any advice I can give you, it's to do the work and face the fears you have. I know you have them. We all do, even if it's hard for guys to talk about them. Why is that? Does being a man mean you're never allowed to be afraid? If that's true, then I've never met a man. Who says you have to be strong all the time? You can laugh and cry and have deep feelings too. That's one thing I always appreciated about you. You were . . . you are never afraid to feel things deeply. Your heart runs wide open. You'll experience great hurt and great love because of it.

And I know it's scary, man, but you can't be afraid of the hurt. The hurt is a risk that comes when you really put another person's heart above your own. When you realize what matters most is not your heart, but someone else's. Being selfless is the highest form of love. That's why I had to let Daisy go.

Maybe now you'll understand why I had to leave. I needed to chase some dreams I thought were long dead. I hope all they need is a little drink and suddenly I'll be in an oasis.

I'll be in touch.

Your friend,
Ezra

I read his letter several times. It's hard to be mad at him when he's being so honest. It's also hard not to miss him.

A little while later, I hear the buzz of talking down the hall. I knock on my mom's door.

"Come in," she calls.

I poke my head in her room. She's on the phone.

"I'll call you later," she says, and ends the call. "Hi, sweetie." She gives me a weak I'm-trying-hard-to-be-positive-for-my-son smile.

"Hi, Mom. Just checking in."

She pats the bed for me to join her. "How was school?"

"Same. How was work?" I ask.

"Same." This time her smile is a little brighter. "Did you see the letter from Ezra?" she asks.

"Yeah."

"Did he go on a trip somewhere?"

"Yeah. He's doing some traveling."

"That's nice. I used to love to travel." She takes in a big breath and lets it out in one big whoosh.

I decide to make something right that has been sitting on my chest since the night I came home from camping. "Mom, I'm sorry for telling you about Dad the way I did."

She holds up her hand. "Neruda, none of this is your fault."

"I know, but I'm talking about the way I blurted it out. I shouldn't have done it like that. It wasn't right."

She nods. "Well, I appreciate the apology."

I don't know what else to say, so I'm starting to get up when her words stop me.

"Neruda, whatever happens with your dad and me, I want you to know that we both love you and that nothing will ever change that."

"I know," I say.

But the knowing doesn't change the fear. The fear that my family will be broken forever.

"Good." She pauses. "You know, love and marriage are complicated. But I don't want you to hate your father."

I can't agree to that yet, so I remain quiet.

"He's still your dad, no matter what he does. And anyone can make mistakes. Remember that, okay?"

She stares at me, waiting for a response.

"Okay," I finally say. "Mom, can I ask you a question?"

"Of course."

"Do you regret it?" I ask.

"Regret what?"

"Marrying Dad."

"Oh no, honey. I love your dad, that's why this is so painful. If I never married your dad, I wouldn't have you." She chokes up a little. "No, I don't have any regrets. I'm just . . . sad and angry and hurt and . . ." She takes a deep breath and pauses as if she realizes that she's sharing too much with me.

I use the pause to ask her another question, even though it's one that I'm not sure I want the answer to. "So does this mean that you guys are getting a divorce?"

She sighs. "We have some things to work out. Big things. I'm not sure what will happen exactly, but I do know that we love each other. That's really all I know right now."

"You still love him after everything?"

She studies her hands. "I love him in spite of everything, I guess."

"I don't get it. I don't understand love at all."

"Love is . . . hard work. People change, grow together, grow apart. I think the real question is whether loving someone is reason enough to forgive the pain they cause you."

I let this sink in, but I don't have an answer.

A little while later, I make both of us some milk and Pepsi. It's Mom's favorite drink when she's sick or feeling blue. She first heard about it on an old TV show called *Laverne and Shirley*. We sit and watch TV together like we used to do when I was a kid.

After Mom turns off her bedroom light, I head out for a late-night walk. I cross through my neighborhood and onto Fig, go south a couple of blocks, and turn down an alley next to a parking lot. I hear a familiar noise, the shaking of a spray can, which draws me deeper into the alley.

The artist, dressed in all black, moves like a shadow, spraying paint on the side of a low brick wall. A flashlight lies on the ground and acts as a spotlight. While I approach as quietly as I can, he bends down and grabs another aerosol can from a white plastic grocery bag near his feet.

He turns suddenly, and for a moment, he looks like a cat about to pounce. He's wearing a face mask to protect against the fumes. The whites of his eyes glow under the soft light. He relaxes when he sees it's only me. He doesn't tell me to leave, so I take that as an invitation. I come closer, stand just a little behind and off to the side, and watch him create a flock of black birds flying across the building. One of them has something in its talons and little drops of blood fall from its grasp.

"You gonna just watch or throw something up yourself?" he says after a while.

"Can I?"

He hands me a similar white mask and points to a clean section of the wall a few paces down.

"You can take that spot over there. I won't get to it tonight. If it sucks, I'll paint over it tomorrow."

"Okay."

I take one of the black cans of paint and shake it. I've used spray paint before, but as fillers, not to do a whole painting. It takes me a few tries to understand the can control. Then I start creating.

After minutes or hours, I don't know which, I feel his eyes on me. I stop and see that he's pulled his mask down, his hands are on his hips, and he's staring at my work.

"Is that original? You didn't copy that from a picture or something?"

"Nah, it's original."

"Cool, man. Tag it."

Uncertain of what my tag should be, I take a red can and sign *ND* underneath the rosebush. I've painted Callie with one of the first faces from her portfolio that she showed me. The one where she had a vine of roses and thorns traveling up her neck and face. For something that I just did on the spot, it looks really good. It's raw, but that's okay because it feels more like a street art piece than what it would look like on canvas. It suits the wall.

I return the cans to the artist. He gives me his card with the name Dante on it and some art studio in LA.

He walks off carrying a plastic bag in each hand.

I examine my portrait of Callie. Her eyes are still not perfect. They are a little sad in this version, like they were the last time I saw her. I note the places that need improvement.

I'm not sure how I feel about having this up in such a public space. I could do better if I practiced it at home and then came back with a polished idea.

But this piece does have something. There's hurt and pain and love and regret. All great emotions I can use to fuel something amazing.

Then I get an idea.

POET'S OBLIGATION

The next day, Luis is standing outside Mr. Nelson's room when I approach. I brace myself for another physical altercation, planning my moves in my mind. I'll have to be quick. Maybe I can smash his face in with my binder before he gets me in one of his fancy pins.

"So, uh, I talked to Mr. Fisher," he says. "I just want you to know there's no hard feelings about yesterday." He holds out his hand.

I assume he's joking, but there is no humor in his eyes. I shake his hand.

"Okay," I say.

"Artistic differences, I get it. Same in wrestling. Everyone's got a signature style. And to be honest, I wasn't really flowing with what we were doing with the mural. It's not bad or anything, just not what I would have designed, you know?"

"Yeah, sure."

Luis steps into the room and I follow him, still slightly unnerved by his apology.

Class begins, and I stare at Callie's empty seat. She doesn't show the whole period.

Mr. Nelson reminds us that our essays are due on Tuesday. I think of asking for an extension because honestly I haven't even started it. Ever since things blew up with Callie, writing a paper on her hasn't been something I'm dying to do. And it's not like I'm going to have tons of time to work on it this weekend, because I have to finish the mural before the unveiling on Monday. I have no idea when or how I'll actually be able to write the paper. Maybe I won't do it. Take an F instead.

With our assignment officially coming to an end, Callie and I won't even have a reason to speak to each other. Not that we're really on speaking terms anyway. I've been trying to avoid her, erase her from my mind, but my actions have only made her a permanent fixture. And I can't shake the memory of her eyes yesterday. She looked upset about something. Now she's not even here.

What did she say? Something about not everything being

about me? Something about other people having things going on?

I stare at her empty chair.

I imagine Callie turning and giving me one of her bored-in-class looks.

It sucks to miss her.

And I realize that the idea of not knowing Callie anymore, of not spending time with her, is worse than her not loving me. I can imagine a world where we are not romantically involved, because that's our world now. But I don't want to imagine one where we are not even friends. I don't want her to become just some stranger I sit next to.

I don't know how to tell her these things, but I wonder if there's a way I can show her.

I spend lunch and Mr. Fisher's class working on the mural. I've finally figured out what I want to add, but I don't have a lot of time and I'm not sure I can do it right.

After the final bell rings, Mr. Fisher comes by to check on my progress. He stares a long time before he pats me on the back.

"Your best work here, Neruda. Really excellent."

"Thanks," I say. And it feels good.

"I'm sorry about Luis," he says, "forcing you two to partner on this. I know it wasn't easy, but you've done a great job."

"Yeah, well, I guess he's not all bad," I say.

I have just two days left to work, so on Saturday, I head to the library for an early start. I paint for hours, only taking a break at 11:00 to go watch some of the volleyball game.

I sneak in and go right to the top bleacher, hoping Callie won't see me. I scan the players, but she isn't in the game. I scan the bench, but she's not there either.

First school, now this. It's not like Callie to miss a game. She's the type to play even if she had pneumonia. After the final game in the set, I approach Imogen.

"Good game," I tell her.

"Thanks!" she says.

"Hey, where's Callie today?"

"She's off the team."

"What?" I don't get it. Callie loves playing volleyball.

Imogen motions for me to lean in. "Her grades got really bad, so she's not allowed to play."

"For good?"

"Not sure. Maybe if she gets them up. We really need her too."

"How is she?"

"You know Callie. She's taking it hard. You should reach out to her. I know you guys are good friends."

Imogen walks back to her teammates, and I head back to the library. It makes sense now why she looked so upset the other day. For Callie not to be on the team anymore, she must be devastated. I had no idea she struggled that much with school. I think about sending her a text, but it seems too little, too late now.

A couple hours later, I finish the mural and carefully put up the sheet. It's not flawless; no art ever is. But I've created something I am proud of.

And I want Callie to see it. I just don't know how to get her there on Monday night.

IT'S GOOD TO FEEL YOU ARE CLOSE TO ME

I wake up Sunday with a feeling of uneasiness gnawing at me. It follows me downstairs, stays with me during breakfast, waits for me outside of the shower. I can't shake it. Normally I'd chalk it up to nerves, but this feels different.

This feels like worry.

Instead of texting or calling, I decide to just show up. If she's home, we're meant to have a conversation. If she isn't home, then I've at least made an attempt to reconcile. Fate will decide either way.

When I pull up to the curb, Callie is outside.

Damn fate.

She's pumping up a bike tire.

"Hi," I say as I cautiously approach her. "You going for a ride?"

"Yep."

"Where?"

"Debs Park."

She finishes the tire and then pumps up the second one.

"Kind of far from here?"

"It's only like three miles."

"I could give you a ride."

"No, thank you. I want the exercise."

When she's done, she stands and attaches the pump back on the bike.

I decide it's now or never, so I ask her, "Do you have plans Monday night?"

"What?"

"There's an unveiling of the mural I've been working on, and I wanted to see if you would come. I mean, if you're free."

She stands there with her arms crossed, looking at me like she wants to throw something. I want to tell her I'm sorry, but she's not making this easy.

"I'll think about it."

"Okay." I turn to leave. Then I turn back around. "Look, I don't know what to say," I blurt out. "I'm sorry."

She doesn't say anything.

I stand there a minute longer, then it's clear I should go. "Okay. Well, have a good ride," I say.

As I'm walking back to my scooter, I hear over my shoulder, "You can use my dad's bike, if you want to come."

"You sure?"

She shrugs and puts on a black helmet with pink flames.

She takes the lead as we bike single file through the streets and past busy intersections. She's right. It isn't that far at all. The problem is when we enter the park, there's a huge, long hill that we have to ride up. Callie doesn't give any indication that she's going to slow down or walk, so I have to work hard to keep up with her. My legs burn as I stand and try to ignore the pain. But I can't stop and walk it. If she can make it, so can I.

I'm all out of breath by the time we reach the actual parking lot and grass fields. Callie stops and takes a drink from her water bottle. I look around for a water fountain. There isn't one.

"Here." Callie throws me the bottle.

"Thanks," I say, and take a drink. I stretch my legs a little so they won't cramp.

"Ready?" she asks.

"Sure," I say, even though I still feel like passing out.

She gets back on her bike and leads us to another hill. This hill is shorter, but it's steeper.

I make it about halfway and then I have to stop.

"It's okay," I croak. "You go on ahead."

Callie doesn't even acknowledge me. She's totally focused. She's a machine. She literally leaves me in her dust.

I push the bike up the rest of the way and take in the view. Downtown LA is on my left. It's a bright, sunny day, so I can see everything super clear. On my right are brown hills and trees and a good deal of Northeast LA.

When I reach the top, Callie is waiting for me. Without a word, she turns to the left, where a small pond sits.

We walk our bikes around the pool of water to a bench on the other side. She props her bike up against a tree and sits down. I do the same and sit next to her, though I'm careful to leave plenty of space between us. We face the relatively still water.

It's shady here and quiet even though we aren't the only ones here. There are some girls in workout clothes on another bench, talking. A guy on the other side of the pond fishes with a small pole.

"Have you been here before?" Callie asks me.

"Once. A long time ago."

"I like to come here and think. Or sometimes when I want to have a Shabbat."

"I thought that was on Saturdays."

"A real Shabbat is. I like the *idea* of Shabbat. A day of rest and remembering and thinking. Every now and then, I just take a day—or, if not a whole day, I take a couple of hours—I turn off my phone, don't go online, and I come here to sit and think. My mom showed me this article where a rabbi talked about how he went to his island of peace during Shabbat. A place where he could be at peace with himself and his family, no matter the situation." She points to the pond. "This is my pond of peace." She smiles.

Callie's right; it is super peaceful here. We sit for a long time and watch the water. Turtles poke their heads out like tiny brown periscopes. Small frogs splash and dart across the top like smooth stones.

She takes a deep breath. "I've been benched."

"Why? What happened?" I pretend not to know anything so that Callie can tell me herself.

"My grades. It's my fault. I know it. I just . . . school is hard for me. Tests and organizing. Remembering to turn in things. That's why I'm in Nelson's English class. I'm not stupid, though, you know?" She looks at me and she is beautiful. She is strong. She is many things, but stupid is not one of them.

"What if your parents talked to your teachers?"

"They were the ones who told my coach I shouldn't be playing until I got my grades up."

"Oh."

"Yeah. Oh."

"So there's no chance of you playing?"

"I mean, there's a tiny chance, I guess." She wipes some tears from her eyes. "I really wanted to go to CIF this year."

"I'm sorry," I say.

And then we don't say anything else. We watch the pond, each in our own thoughts. The nervousness I felt at being so close to her, the smell of her, the beauty, begins to fade. The question of why she didn't kiss me back, which was so prominent in my mind, I push aside. I remember that I enjoy simply being with her.

I look down at her hand, the one with the elephant ring on it. I take a risk and reach for it, squeeze it, and then let go. I don't need to hold on to it to love her. And just because she didn't kiss me back doesn't mean I can't keep loving her either.

Maybe Ezra is right. Maybe love is knowing when to hold on and when to let go.

Sometimes love is just showing up.

Sometimes love looks like sitting quietly, watching a pond.

And I can do that.

I DO NOT LOVE YOU EXCEPT BECAUSE I LOVE YOU

I pull at the knot of the tie Mom made me add to my ensemble, one of Dad's skinny black ones. I thought I was fine in a button-down light-blue shirt and jeans, but Mom said this is a big night and I needed to be more formal. If I knew formal would feel like I was being choked every time I turned my head, I would have ditched the tie in the car.

Mr. Fisher works the small foyer. I'm actually surprised at how many people showed up. Most are adults I don't recognize. But Greyson is here too with other guys from our art class. He gives me the thumbs-up sign. Everyone's buzzing about the LOVE IS wall.

I stand next to the covered mural and politely shake the hands of people Mr. Fisher introduces me to. They're from the school board, the community, and a few artist friends of his. I try to smile and focus on their faces, but I keep looking over shoulders, around talking heads, scanning the crowd for another face.

She isn't here.

Mom and Dad stand next to each other and appear to be talking. To any outside observer, it would seem that they are a typical married couple, but their body language speaks of the unresolve between them. Dad hasn't touched her once. He has his hands in his pockets, and Mom's arms are crossed in front of her.

Mr. Fisher calls for everyone's attention and the crowd quiets down. The first person to speak is Mr. Jones, our principal. He gives a general welcome and then says how proud he is of Mr. Fisher and his contribution to our school. He keeps talking, but I don't have a clue what he's saying because I glance toward the back and see Callie standing there. Her hair is up in two little buns on the side, and she's wearing a black dress and a purple cardigan. She gives me a head nod when she sees me. I barely nod back. I can't look too eager. Besides, now I'm nervous.

I hear my name and suddenly Mr. Fisher is talking about the mural and about me, and then it's my turn to speak.

"Thank you, Mr. Fisher, and everyone who has come out tonight." I pause, trying to remember what else I'm supposed to say. "Uh, so the mural was designed to be a reflection of our student body. How different and similar we all are. How we're all a part of this collective experience of school, and it's a part of us too. I hope you like it."

Mr. Fisher moves to stand at the opposite end of the sheet curtain as me. This is it. The biggest, most important art piece I've ever done. Years from now, I hope I'll be able to look back on this as the beginning of my professional art career. People will say this is where the artist Neruda Diaz got his start.

Mr. Fisher encourages the crowd to count.

"One! Two! Three!"

Together we pull the sheet off the wall.

I back away from it and examine my work.

It's as if all the air has been sucked out of the room. Then I hear low rumblings that become small tremors. Someone giggles. The rumbling becomes louder. Mr. Fisher puts his hand on my shoulder and squeezes it hard.

"What? Did you . . . ?" He looks into my surprised eyes and he knows that I most certainly did not have anything to do with what we're looking at. Well, I did, but not the parts that everyone is freaking out about.

The mural has eight different students on it. A boy and a

girl embracing underneath a tree. Two guys playing with a soccer ball. A girl sitting and reading a book on some steps. The prominent girl in the front, who looks a lot like Callie, stares off in the distance. A boy skates with his backpack slung over his shoulder. A girl walks and strums a guitar. I created all of them.

What I didn't create is the genitalia that has been drawn over each of them in thick black marker. The girls have huge melon boobs. The boys all have drooping penises and extra-large balls.

I find Callie's eyes in the crowd and they're wide in shock, like everyone else's.

This was supposed to be my moment.

"Excuse me, everyone," Mr. Fisher says. "I am very sorry, but as you can see, this beautiful mural has been vandalized and defaced. I apologize for the graphic images. We will get to the bottom of this and the responsible party will be held accountable."

I know who did it. I would recognize his artistry anywhere. No wonder he was cool with me earlier. I should have known.

From now on, everyone will associate my name with this stupid mural. Instead of "Neruda, like the poet?" they'll say, "Oh yeah, that artist, the one who did the mural with the boobs and floating penises?"

I back away from the wall and the library and all of the

people looking at me with concern. Callie and I lock eyes, but I can't look at her for more than a second. Even she cannot console me.

I walk outside and keep going until my mom pulls up alongside me and gives me a ride home.

POESIA

The following day, I find out Luis has been suspended. Even if it doesn't change what happened, it does make me feel a bit better.

But English class quickly destroys whatever sense of peace I've found, because Mr. Nelson begins by telling us to take out our papers.

"I thought it would be fun to hear from you guys today. See what you wrote about your partners. That way, we can all learn a little something more about each other."

He calls on Josh and Shannon to go first. I don't hear what they're saying because my heart is pounding in my head. I didn't know he was going to make us read them out loud. I read and reread what I wrote over the weekend, which was barely anything. After the disaster with the mural, I couldn't really concentrate on writing.

Callie is silent next to me, with only the occasional clanging of her bracelets like a quiet ripple across a pond. I try to steal a glance at her paper, but she has it covered. I can only make out the title: *The Enigma of Neruda Diaz*. She kept it the same.

After a few pairs read their essays, Mr. Nelson calls on me and Callie. She looks at me to go first.

"Callie Leibowitz sat next to me for thirty-nine days, took approximately 897,001 breaths, before I noticed she had eyes like the ocean. I don't mean the color. Anyone can look and see that her eyes are light brown. I mean if you look too long, you'll start to drift off on one of the currents, and you'll see how she's much more than who she appears to be, sitting here in class in those beat-up black boots of hers.

"Here's what I've learned about Callie.

"She was born in Huntington Hospital seventeen years ago. She's always lived in the same house. It's about a mile and a half from here. Her parents are still together, which doesn't seem like a big thing, but it is. They're nice. Her dad is very tall. She looks like a younger version of her mom. She has a yellow dog named Lucy. Lucy smells like old, worn socks because she's probably not bathed enough, but I haven't said anything to Callie about this. It's just something I've observed."

I stop reading because this is where I stopped writing.

How do I talk about Callie's essence? How do I capture on the page what is essentially untranslatable? It would be just as hard as explaining how the stars hang in the sky or how a cheetah blurs across an African desert or how a blade of grass grows from the ground. All of these things are beautiful and unique and totally unto themselves and speak of something deep and unknowable, as if to even attempt to explain them would reduce them, make them less somehow.

"Mr. Nelson, I'm not very good with words, as you know. If I can, I'd like to show you."

"What do you mean?" Mr. Nelson asks.

"The rest of my essay." I stand up. "I'd like to show it to you. Can the class please follow me?"

He raises his eyebrows at me, probably deciding if he's going to let me do this or not. "All right. Everyone up. Quiet in the halls. Neruda, this was not the assignment. It better be good."

I walk out of the classroom, leading the class into the quad and over to the library. The graffiti has already been cleaned off for the most part. There are still some faint lines left, and you can make out the images that had been there. I can repaint the spots that were damaged. I can also redo some sections that I wasn't super pleased with.

But it doesn't matter.

Now the mural is totally my own.

After everyone enters, I say, "Someone tried to destroy my mural. So I have to fix it in places, but hopefully you can look past that."

I point to the portrait of the prominent girl in the front who is staring off in the distance. The girl who looks like Callie because she is Callie.

"This is the rest of my essay. I tried to capture the core of who Callie is." *And what she means to me,* I want to say, but I don't say the last part aloud. I stand back and invite them to look at it.

Everyone is quiet. It's like we're in some sacred space. They take turns standing in front of the portrait of Callie before moving aside and waiting by the front door.

I watch Callie, but her expression is unreadable.

Mr. Nelson is the last to face the wall. He stands there awhile before he turns to me. Finally he smiles, and I swear there are tears in his eyes.

As we're walking back to class, I get a lot of positive comments about the mural. I also get sympathy regarding the damage done. It's surprising how decent people can be sometimes.

But the one person I want to hear from most doesn't say a word. She hurries out of class without a word or a glance in my direction.

At home after school, I'm surprised to find Dad there. He's on a stepladder on the porch, unscrewing the burnt-out bulb.

"Hey, Neruda," he says when I approach.

"Hey."

"Finally changing the bulb here." He gives it one more twist and removes the bulb. "Help me out?" He hands it to me.

I take the old bulb. He points to the new one in the package on the ground. I grab it and give it to him. He twists it in, gets off the ladder, and turns on the switch. The bulb shines brightly above us.

"Good as new."

He folds up the ladder and walks it back to the garage. He comes out rolling his bike.

"I forgot this the other day." He brings it to his car and leans it against the side. "So, how was the fallout today?"

I shrug. "They've already cleaned most of it off the wall."

"I'm sorry that happened to you, son." He moves his hand toward me like he's going to touch my arm, but he drops it instead. "And I'm sorry this has been such a hard time. It's not what I would have wished on anyone." Tears well up in his eyes, and I turn away, embarrassed by them.

"How's your mom doing?" he asks.

"Good." I'm not sure what their arrangement is, but I don't want to be the middleman. If he wants to know what's going on with her, he needs to ask her.

"How's Tía Lilia?" I ask.

"Busy. I've hardly seen her. But her place is nice. You'll have to come over soon. We can do dinner."

"Yeah, sure," I say. And I guess this is how it's going to be for a while. I'll see my dad randomly and on weekends. It sucks.

I'm about to head inside when my dad says, "Want to play?"

"What?"

He points to the hoop in our driveway. I can't remember the last time Dad and I played hoops together. We used to play all the time when I was younger.

"Just a game or two. I mean, if you have time."

I want to tell him I don't. But there's also a part of me that wants things to be okay between us, to know that we can get back some of what we've lost and get to a place where we can move forward. So I say yes.

I get the ball from the garage and toss it to Dad.

As he's dribbling, I steal the ball from him and quickly do a layup. It goes in.

"That's one."

"Okay, okay," he says. "Don't get cocky. We play to twenty-one."

We don't talk much for the rest of the game. Or during the second one, except to call out fouls. I play hard, and so does Dad. In the end, each of us is both a winner and a loser, and that's okay by me.

THE WIDE OCEAN

"Neruda!" Mom yells. "Can you get the door?"

When I open it, Callie is standing there.

"Oh, hi," I say.

"Hi."

She looks so pretty with her pink top and jeans rolled half-way up her ankles.

I look around and see her bike parked in our driveway.

"You biked here?" I ask, though I shouldn't be surprised.

"Yeah. Can you take a walk?" she asks.

I follow her out to the street, where we turn right and walk around the block. It's cooler now that it's early evening, but I start to sweat. I take her through the neighborhood, wondering how long we are going to walk like this. Maybe I should just start talking about something, but the words we don't say pile up between us.

"I thought you said you were going to give me a copy of the drawing you made at LACMA," she says. "I didn't expect to see it on the library wall."

"I didn't know how to talk to you after, you know . . ."

"I know," she says. "Me neither. It's just that I've been really burned in the past by guys—well, one guy really—and I just feel like I need to focus on me. Figure out my own stuff, you know?"

And there it is. The truth.

"I'm sorry. I didn't handle things well," she continues.

"Maybe we both didn't," I say softly. "I didn't mean to make you feel weird. With the mural. I just wanted you to see how I see you. But you know, Luis added his artistic embellishments."

"Yeah, about that. The proportions were all off, don't you think?"

"What?"

"My boobs are not that big."

I stare at her, careful to keep my eyes on her face.

"Too soon?" she asks.

"Probably."

"Luis is a jerk. And it sucks what he did. I'm sorry."

I nod. "I can paint it over," I say. "But thank you."

"You're welcome."

She smiles and I feel the air lighten.

"So, do you think we can do this?" she asks. "Be friends again?"

She's asking me to get past the kiss, to change my expectations, to be her friend.

It's not what I would choose first, but I'm happy I get a choice.

"It depends," I say.

"On what?"

"As long as I get to pick the movies sometimes."

We turn down another street and keep walking. We're traveling farther and farther from my house now. The sun is shifting in the sky, casting long shadows behind us.

"But you don't know anything about movies," she says. Callie goes off on how she's much more of a movie expert than I am, how that gives her a credibility that I don't have. How it's in both our best interests if she picks the movies, most of the time.

I fall in step to the rhythm of her voice. The more she talks, the more my faith in love begins to grow again. For a moment I close my eyes and picture hers and I'm drawn back into the deep, but her voice is there as well, steady, and it keeps me above the current. It guides me like a lighthouse back to the shore and speaks to my deepest parts and whispers, "You are not alone."

You are not alone moves in and out, in and out with the tide of her voice.

Callie's eyes turn toward me all lit up because she's telling me about the latest movie that she's going to show me.

I gaze into her horizon and I know that this is enough.

For now.

This is enough.

ACKNOWLEDGMENTS

Thank you, Esteban Payan, who first introduced me to Pablo Neruda when you were my student way back when. Who knew it would be the catalyst for a life of reading his work and a future book?

Thank you to the following people who helped me with some details along the way: Franco Gonzalez, August Many, Jakob Williams, Jason Takarabe, and Jordan Dokolas.

Thank you, Liza Kaplan, for championing Neruda from the beginning and for helping me get his story where it needed to be. Thanks to Talia Benamy and the rest of the crew at Philomel. I am so happy to be part of team Philomel.

Thank you, Kerry Sparks. Your praises are many and easy to sing.

Thank you to my family. David, I love you. Aiden, Matisse, and Judah, you are my joy. Now, go read some books!